GODZILLA™

A novelization by H.B. Gilmour

Based on the screenplay written by
Dean Devlin & Roland Emmerich

SCHOLASTIC INC.
New York   Toronto   London   Auckland   Sydney

GODZILLA™

JUNE 1968...

On a small island in the Pacific, a lizard stirred.

Driven by hunger, the six-foot-long reptile crawled from its nest.

Reluctantly leaving its eggs exposed, the creature moved cautiously out of the jungle and started across the warm sand to the sea.

The big lizard stopped suddenly. Sensing danger, it paused at the water's edge, suspiciously sniffing the air. Its alert yellow eyes shifted nervously.

Something was wrong.

The lizard turned abruptly and scurried back into the steamy underbrush, hoping to protect its nest against the mysterious dark force.

Moments later a squadron of French bombers roared over the island.

A missile shrieked to earth, exploding on impact.

The sky went blindingly white.

Then everything turned dark.

From a gigantic mushroom cloud, deadly flakes of nuclear ash drifted down onto what was left of the little island.

The fiery explosion had incinerated the thick jungle.

The sparkling sand across which the big lizard had skittered was now a beach of boiling gray ash.

Toxic debris, many inches thick, covered the remains of the creature and began to smother the nest it had tried to protect.

Only one egg remained.

Into its damaged shell seeped the suffocating fumes the French nuclear bomb test had unleashed.

MORE THAN TWENTY YEARS LATER...

The storm came up suddenly in the gray dawn, violently stirring the sea. Waves fifty feet high crashed onto the deck of the *Kobayashi Maru*.

The Japanese ship, a floating fish factory, was full and ready to return to port. In its hold, hundreds of pounds of silver and yellow tuna glistened in giant metal containers.

The Pacific's wild turbulence did not trouble the ship's skipper. After several uneventful days at sea, he was bored. Watching sumo wrestling on TV, his drowsy eyes fought to stay open. But he was almost asleep.

The blare of a sonar warning, loud and shrill, startled him. The skipper's head jerked up. His eyes flew open. On the sonar screen, he saw something enormous heading directly for the ship.

"Captain," he called, hitting the intercom button. "This is the bridge. We have an emergency."

Alarms blared throughout the *Kobayashi Maru*. The crew rushed from its quarters into cramped gangways that stank of fish. Sliding on the oily floors in their hip-high rubber boots, they raced for the upper decks.

"What's going on?" the ship's elderly cook called from the galley doorway.

A moment ago he'd been hacking vegetables, preparing fish soup for the crew. He'd been humming an old Japanese sea chanty. It was a song about Gojira, the fierce dragon that lurked beneath the waves.

The cook was nervous. Now seamen rushed past him. Metal stairways clanged beneath their pounding feet. The alarm horn sounded deafeningly.

The old man reached out, trying to catch one of the racing men. "What is happening?!" he shrilly demanded.

Before anyone could answer, the *Kobayashi Maru* was rocked by an enormous thud. Something slammed into its hull.

The men in the passageway were tossed against the steel walls and slick decks. The frightened cook tried to hang onto the galley door for balance as the immense ship swayed treacherously.

A second blow rocked the vessel, throwing the stunned old man to the floor.

"What was that?!" he heard the captain's voice scream through the intercom.

A barrage of whistling squawks and static followed. Then someone responded over the speakers, "We must have hit something."

Holding onto the bolted legs of his worktable, the cook tried to scramble to his feet. Another thump jarred the ship. Screams erupted in the hallway. A gush of seawater washed into the galley from the corridor, carrying with it two horrified seamen desperately scrabbling for a foothold.

Raw fear propelled the aproned old man. He scrambled over the struggling seamen and dove out into the hallway. No sooner had he landed, sprawled and flapping like one of the fish stuffed in the ship's hold, than an earsplitting sound erupted.

Before him, the steel wall of the ship crumpled. What

looked like, *but could not have been,* enormous claws began puncturing the metal like immense can openers.

"Gojira!" the cook screamed.

Water flooded through the monstrous gashes. The *Kobayashi Maru* tilted wildly, throwing the cook against the torn wall.

Ducking under the cavernous yellow claws, the cook half-swam and half-clambered toward the stairs. Chased by rising seawater and driven by terror, he climbed for his life.

What awaited him when he reached the top deck was a creature beyond imagining. More monstrous than the old seaman's most violent nightmare, it reared up out of the ocean and lunged at the bridge of the doomed fishing ship.

The next day, on the tiny South Pacific island of Tahiti, a line of black cars sped along the coastal highway. The sea was vast and green on one side of the road, the jungle dark and tangled on the other.

Ten minutes later, the caravan screeched to a stop in front of the Papeete Hospital. Doors slammed. A group of men in lightweight linen suits hurried toward the hospital entrance.

Many of the men were gripping briefcases. Some, however, carried video and sound equipment. A thin man with a camera on his shoulder was almost knocked over by a young Frenchman who was rushing from the building.

"*Pardon,*" Jean-Claude, the young Frenchman, murmured without stopping. Running a hand nervously through his hair, he caught up with the group of men. They all entered the hospital. "We've been getting pressure from the Americans," he blurted out in French.

"What have you told them?" The man who appeared to be in charge was wearing dark glasses. His hair was cut close to his skull. Its blue-black bristles looked as rough as sandpaper. Traces of gray speckled his short dark beard.

"Nothing, Phillipe," Jean-Claude assured the man, pulling open a door for him.

"Are there any others?" Phillipe demanded, stepping out of the car. He was dressed in a pale tan linen suit. "Any other survivors?" he snapped at Jean-Claude, who hurried alongside him.

"Only the one," the young Frenchman responded, following Phillipe into the building. "He was very lucky."

Racing down the corridor ahead of them were the men with the briefcases, cameras, and audio gear. They stopped in front of a room at the end of the hall.

A native Tahitian stood guard outside the room.

Jean-Claude pushed through the waiting men. With a nod to the guard, he opened the door and Phillipe entered.

In a tall white bed, shaking, curled up with his knees to his chin, was the cook from the *Kobayashi Maru*.

Two doctors and three nurses attended the shivering old man. "Get them out of there," Phillipe snapped.

As Jean-Claude ushered the medical staff out, Phillipe signaled to his men. They rushed into the room and began to unpack and set up their recording equipment.

Phillipe moved closer to the old cook. Then he turned to one of the briefcase bearers, a tall, nervous-looking young man. "Jean-Luc," he snapped, "ask him what happened."

In rapid Japanese, Jean-Luc began quizzing the frail patient. But the quivering cook did not respond.

"It's no use." Jean-Luc shrugged sadly. "Whatever happened to him on that ship put him in a complete state of shock."

Phillipe patted his coat pocket. Taking out a slim silver lighter, he flicked it on and held it in front of the stunned cook's dead eyes.

Slowly, the small, dark eyes flickered back to life.

"What did you see, old man?" Phillipe coaxed, bringing the blue light closer to the old cook's face.

A new bout of shivering wracked the ancient seaman. "Gojira!" he shouted suddenly. "GOJIRA!"

The rusty van raced through the rain. Gripping the steering wheel, Dr. Niko Tatopoulos, "Nick" to his friends, squinted through the windshield at the gloomy Russian landscape.

The van's wipers could barely clear away the torrent of water assaulting it. But inside, his spirits undampened by the foul weather, Nick sang along to music blaring from the headphones of his Walkman.

The old truck rattled down a narrow street, then raced past a roadblock. Nailed to the barrier was a sign announcing in Russian: NO TRESPASSING! NUCLEAR RADIATION!

Ahead, the tower of the Chernobyl power plant became visible. Beating out a jaunty rhythm on the steering wheel, Nick squinted through the windshield at the site of one of the world's worst nuclear disasters.

In the shadow of the deserted plant, the van came to a stop. Shouting more than singing along to the Walkman, Nick hopped out and stared at a muddy field nearby. Then he opened the van's rear doors and took out three metal suitcases.

The rain continued. Nick, unconcerned with the nasty weather, set the metal cases down on the puddled ground and opened one.

His hair was wet, plastered in soaked strings to his head. Brushing it out of his eyes, Nick studied the assortment of scientific equipment in the case.

A handful of photographs were taped inside the lid, pictures of a pretty blue-eyed girl with curly blond hair. There were also a couple of snapshots of a slightly younger and much drier Nick looking happy with her.

He glanced at the photos, then pulled from his case two long cables with large spikes attached to the ends.

Hurrying over to the rain-soaked field, Nick shoved the spikes into the mud. A moment later, dozens of worms were crawling up out of the black ooze, huge, plump, and very agitated.

Audrey, the blond in the snapshots, had been right, Nick thought as he kneeled in the mud. His life would have bored her. Here he was, for instance, in a slimy field in the midst of a Russian downpour, checking the results of radioactivity on Chernobyl earthworms.

Some people would call that boring, he guessed. Some would call it crazy. But for him, it was a chance to investigate and possibly do something about the effects of nuclear fallout on living creatures.

From his case, Nick grabbed a large glass jar and began filling it with the oversized worms.

"I'm singin' in the mud, just scooping up my worms," he sang.

Between his own voice and the music booming through his headphones, he didn't hear the Russian military helicopter landing behind him.

The big chopper set down a few feet from the van. Only the intense wind kicked up by its whirling blades and the spray of mud it sent in Nick's direction finally caught his attention.

He glanced over his shoulder. Scrambling to his feet, he was shocked to see several Russian officers hurrying toward him.

"Good day," he recited, trying to remember the right Russian words. "I am . . . er, here with permission," he struggled on in broken Russian. "I have a . . . a . . ." Finally, shifting his jar of worms and searching through his pockets, he said in English, "Permit. I have it here somewhere. How do you say 'permit'?"

"Dr. Niko Topopolosis?" an American voice shouted over the noise of the hovering helicopter.

Nick looked up. As the Russian soldiers moved past him, hurrying toward his equipment cases, a tall man in a long raincoat stepped forward.

"It's Tatopoulos," Nick corrected him.

"The worm guy, right?" the man in the raincoat said, extending his hand. "I'm with the U.S. State Department."

The Russian soldiers packed up Nick's equipment and started carrying his cases toward the helicopter.

"Hey," Nick called out, annoyed at the interruption. "Where are you going? What are they doing?" he asked.

"You've just been reassigned," the tall American replied.

A FISHING VILLAGE IN PANAMA

It was not raining in Panama. Sunshine reflected like sequins off every wave in the harbor.

Dozens of boats filled with frantic reporters bobbed in the choppy waters. Video cameras rolling, they called out questions. Their words were lost in the racket of helicopters overhead, and police boats patrolling the harbor, and U.S. military trucks rumbling along the docking pier.

"Dr. Niko Topodopeless?" a forceful voice demanded.

Nick blinked at the American military man marching up the

pier toward him. Colonel Alex Hicks offered the thinnest trace of a welcoming smile.

"It's Tatopoulos," Nick corrected the colonel.

"Whatever. Can someone get those people out of here?!" Hicks shouted, gesturing at the unruly press corps. Then he put a solid hand on Nick's back and scooped him along, away from the chaotic harbor.

"Where are we? What is this place?" Nick asked as they left the pier and started down a rutted dirt road.

"Fishing village," said Hicks, walking faster now. "Anyway, it used to be."

"Excuse me," Nick said, wringing out the wrist of his still-damp sweatshirt, "would you mind telling me what I'm doing here?"

The dirt road veered into the jungle. Hicks moved along it swiftly, with long, deliberate strides. "You wouldn't believe me if I told you, Tatooplus," he replied over his shoulder, disappearing into a thick stand of palm trees and knee-high grass.

Before Nick could say, "Just call me Nick," he had followed the colonel into a clearing filled with debris.

It took him a moment to realize that he was looking at the shattered remains of a village.

"What happened here?" he asked.

A few splintered houses still stood, their corrugated roofs crushed and hanging askew. A tangle of fishing net hung weirdly from the top of a tree. Caught in its ropes, a handful of fish dangled helplessly. More fish littered the ground under the tree.

Military tents and a small medical station were set up near a collapsed building. Civilians, some in white uniforms, and combat-ready soldiers combed the ruins. Nick heard the clicking of a Geiger counter nearby. "Was it a radiation spill?" he asked.

"Something like that," Hicks replied, stepping around a tin roof that lay on the ground. It was dented in the center, as if a giant fist had karate-chopped it.

"Look, I work for the Nuclear Regulatory Commission, but accidents and spills are not my field," Nick protested, hurrying after the colonel.

"We know," Hicks said, motioning to some guards, who cleared away a blockade from the jungle pathway. "Come on," he ordered, ducking under a low hanging vine and taking the narrow trail.

"Do you know that you just interrupted a three-year study of the Chernobyl earthworm?" Nick demanded, following Hicks down a shallow slope in the jungle floor.

"Sure," Hicks said. "You're the worm guy."

"The worm guy? Yeah, I'm the worm guy," Nick said, annoyed. "Did you know that radioactive contamination in that area has mutated the earthworm's DNA? Do you have any *idea* what that means?"

"No," Hicks said evenly, stepping over a rotting fish carcass, "but I have a feeling I'm about to find out."

"It means," Nick said, hurrying to keep up with the military man, "that due to a man-made accident at a Russian nuclear plant, Chernobyl earthworms are now over seventeen percent larger than they were before!"

Hicks stopped and turned to Nick. "Really?" he said. But he didn't seem very impressed. A strange smile creased his thin lips. "Sounds big."

"Big? They're enormous!" Nick persisted. "That's what I've

been trying to tell you. I'm a biologist. I monitor the effect of radiation on organisms. I take radioactive samples and I study them," Nick said, frustrated.

"Great," Hicks said. He pointed to the ground. "Here's your sample. Study it," he said and walked away.

Nick looked down. All he saw were his own muddy high-tops planted on the worn jungle floor. "What sample?" he called to Colonel Hicks.

"You're standing in it," Hicks responded, climbing back up the pit they stood in without turning around.

Nick looked down again. He saw earth. Crushed vegetation. Flattened grass. Another fish lay splattered on the ground. Insects fed on it. "I don't see it!" he shouted to the colonel's retreating back.

Then he noticed two men in white uniforms spreading out a tape measure along the sides of the jungle basin.

Two other men were moving across the sunken clearing with Geiger counters. Through the distant muffled racket of the harbor with its boats and helicopters, and the surrounding sounds of the jungle, Nick was suddenly aware that the Geiger counters were clicking loudly and continuously.

He turned slowly.

For the first time, he saw that he was standing inside a shallow crater, an indentation in the jungle floor that looked about fifteen yards long. It was like a short, sunken football field.

Or a giant footprint in the earth.

And all along its far ridge, radiation-detection devices were clicking.

Ahead, through an area of downed trees and crushed bushes, he saw another crater. In that one, too, men with Geiger counters were walking, measuring what seemed like an unusually high amount of radiation.

Scrambling up out of the crater, Nick stared ahead. Five similar holes were stamped into the earth.

"No," he breathed. "It can't be. It's not possible."

Ten minutes later, he tore back into the devastated village. Skirting the crushed tin roof, he rushed to catch up with Colonel Hicks, who was heading for the command tent.

"That was a footprint!" Nick shouted.

The colonel turned to him and, smiling now, nodded.

"I was standing *inside* a footprint!" Nick said.

"That's right," Hicks agreed, moving toward the tent again.

A woman in jungle fatigues, with curly red hair, was waiting in front of the tent. She was holding a clipboard. She tapped it impatiently while she studied Nick.

"But there is no animal in the world that can make footprints like that," he was saying to Colonel Hicks. He paused. "Is there?"

"I told them this is not your field," the redhead announced. "But no one listens to genius."

Nick looked up. "Dr. Elsie Chapman," the woman introduced herself. "Head of the research team."

"Dr. Chapman is with the National Institute of Paleontology," Hicks explained. "She's your boss."

Paleontology? As he shook Elsie Chapman's hand, Nick's mind raced.

What did studying fossils, the imprints of creatures that had lived millions of years ago, have to do with the destruction of this village?

Did the military actually believe that a *dinosaur* had come stomping through Panama in search of a fish dinner?

The footprints, if that was what they truly were, had been made recently. A day or so ago at most.

"Those *are* footprints, right?" Nick asked again. And when

Elsie nodded and said, "Looks like it," he added, "Did anyone see what made them?"

"No such luck," she said.

"It happened so fast, no one knew what hit them until it was over," Hicks explained.

"Footprints?" Nick shook his head. "You don't think . . ." he began.

But Elsie was no longer listening. She and the colonel were staring at a Jeep that had just pulled up. "There's Craven," she said.

"I've got it. The tape's in," a stout man with a red nose and watery eyes called to them. Waving a canvas courier's bag stamped TOP SECRET, and sneezing violently, he scrambled out of the Jeep.

"The French finally released it," he told Hicks. Dabbing at his raw nose with a handkerchief, he sprinted past the colonel and, with Elsie Chapman at his heels, hurried into the command tent.

"Sorry, summer cold. Weired, huh?" Dr. Craven said.

The huge tent was packed with electronic and scientific equipment. "Over here, Dr. Craven." A man in a white lab coat took the canvas bag and rushed it over to a video player.

"A Japanese cannery ship was attacked and sunk yesterday," Colonel Hicks told Nick as they hurried toward the TV monitor. "It was near the French Polynesians."

Elsie said, "We think there's a connection."

Nick tried to picture the area, tried to remember exactly where French Polynesia was. In the Pacific Ocean, he knew.

It was a series of tiny islands in the Pacific, about three thousand miles east of Australia, he thought.

And nearly five thousand miles west of Panama.

"A connection?" he said aloud. "What kind of connection?"

"Dr. Craven," Elsie changed the subject with a chuckle, "have you met our worm guy? Tootupolus, this is Mendel Craven."

"Tatopoulos," Nick murmured as the TV went on. "Please. Call me Nick."

"Holy cow," said Mendel Craven. "What happened to that guy?"

Nick stared at the screen.

On a white hospital bed, a shrunken old man was rocking back and forth, repeating the same word over and over.

It sounded like *Go-jeed-ah*.

"Gojira," the old man chanted. "Gojira . . . Gojira!"

"Gojira?" Elsie repeated. "What's Gojira?" she demanded. "What does that mean?"

The yellow cab pulled up in front of the WIDF-TV studios in New York City. Audrey Timmonds paid the driver and picked up the grocery bags on the seat beside her.

This was her lucky day, Audrey told herself. She had actually found a taxi in the middle of a thunderstorm during rush hour in Manhattan.

Arms filled with groceries, she slid out of the cab into the pelting rain.

This was the day she'd been waiting for. Today she was going to be promoted from Charles Caiman's assistant to on-camera news reporter.

Definitely.

If her boss kept his promise.

Which he never did.

Think positively, she reminded herself as two desperate New Yorkers ran at her, ready to do battle for the empty cab.

Audrey jumped out of their way into an ankle-deep puddle. But not even ruining the new shoes she'd spent half a week's salary on, or the fact that her thick blond hair was soaked beneath her beret, was going to shake her confidence.

Something *big* was going to happen today.

It had to, Audrey thought, sloshing through the revolving doors of the WIDF building. After all, she'd come to New York straight out of college to be a news reporter. Not a coffee-making, script-typing, lunch-ordering, phone-answering, grocery-buying research assistant.

On the twelfth floor, Audrey's best friend, Lucy, was working feverishly at her computer. Glancing up, she saw Audrey lurching through the busy office.

"What's all this?" Lucy asked.

"Caiman's groceries." Audrey couldn't hide her anger about her job responsibilities.

"Oh, girl," Lucy said sympathetically. Then, looking past Audrey, she murmured, "Speak of the devil."

Charles Caiman was WIDF's nightly news anchor. He was not an impressive-looking man in person. Actually, he was kind of short and sleazy. "Height-impaired," Lucy called him. "A legend in his own mind."

Audrey, who had only seen Caiman on television before she started working at the station, had been surprised at how squat and self-involved he was. Smiling behind the news desk, decked out in a designer suit with his hair sprayed to crackling stiffness, he had seemed so . . . *trustworthy*.

He wasn't smiling now. He was studying his script, the one Audrey had written an hour ago.

Mumbling and gesturing dramatically, Caiman strutted past them, heading for the studio at the back of the office.

"Luce, should I ask him?" Audrey whispered nervously.

"No," Lucy whispered through clenched teeth.

But then Audrey remembered it was her lucky day. "I'm going to ask," she announced, bolting after the anchorman despite Lucy's protest.

Caiman looked up, saw her, and started walking faster.

"Mr. Caiman," Audrey called. "Hey! Hi." She caught up with him. "Did you talk with Humphries?"

"Audrey, Audrey." Without stopping, Caiman shook his groomed head impatiently. "This is not the place —"

"Just tell me," she said, hurrying alongside him. "Did you ask him? You promised you'd tell him how well I've been doing. You know, how I research all your best stories and write your scripts —"

"*Assist* me in writing my scripts," Caiman corrected her.

She didn't argue. Leaning against the wall was a big cardboard cutout of the WIDF news team, with a smiling Charles Caiman standing front and center.

The life-sized poster wobbled as Audrey brushed by it. "But you told him, right?" she said, steadying the shaky cutout. "You told him that I'm ready —"

But Caiman wasn't ready. He wasn't even listening.

Audrey cleared her throat and tried again. "Mr. Caiman," she said, "I've been doing extra research for you after hours and weekends for over three years —"

"I'd love to stay and chat," Caiman interrupted her, "but it's time for the grown-ups to go to work. Now, if you'll excuse me?" he said sarcastically, pushing past her and into the studio.

Through the glass, Audrey watched him size up his new co-anchor, who was about six inches taller than him.

"Box!" he hollered. A stagehand rushed over and set an apple crate down next to the newsman. Audrey watched Caiman climb up onto it.

He was the same height as his co-anchor now. A satisfied smile slid across his face.

Turning away in disgust, Audrey came face-to-face with the cardboard cutout. Taking out her gum, she stuck it on the newsman's nose.

GREAT PEDRO BLUFF, JAMAICA

The Jeep bumped along a winding road. Nick sat wedged in the backseat between his boss, Elsie, and the sneezing Dr. Mendel Craven.

"Three years digging up worms in Chernobyl?" Elsie said. "How did Mrs. Tatopoulos handle that?"

"Oh, I'm not married," Nick explained.

"A girlfriend, then?" the paleontologist persisted.

For a moment, Nick thought of Audrey. "Not for a long time now," he said as the Jeep pulled onto a beach guarded by soldiers.

A small crowd ringed the area that the military had roped off. A TV crew was already on the scene, shouting questions.

"Clear these people out of here." Colonel Hicks climbed out of the Jeep in front of Nick's. With his aides and the scientists jogging after him, he pushed through the onlookers.

Mendel gasped.

"What in the world?" Elsie muttered.

Nick stared, speechless.

Taking up nearly the entire beach, a huge cargo ship lay on its side in the sand. There were gigantic holes ripped into its hull.

Three men were taking measurements of the jagged holes.

"Who are those guys?" Colonel Hicks demanded as the scientists started toward the ship. "Lieutentant, get them away from there."

"They are with me." The man with the short gray-black beard and close-cropped hair removed his dark glasses. "Phillipe Roache, Colonel." He handed Hicks a business card. "La Rochelle, property and casualty insurance," he recited in thick, French-accented English. "I am the agent in charge. We are preparing a report."

"You're fast," Colonel Hicks grumbled.

"That is our job," Phillipe said, smiling coldly.

"Well, your people are getting in the way of my job." Hicks pushed past the agent.

A few feet from the beached ship, at the edge of the sand, Nick noticed a torn crate of tuna fish. There were several more cans scattered in the sand.

Mendel was examining the cargo ship's hull for radiation. The clicking of his Geiger counter caught Nick's attention. He hurried back to the ship and began to examine the gashes in its side.

There was something stuck to the largest rip, something that looked like raw steak.

Nick took off his knapsack and searched through it until he found the sterile jar and pair of tweezers he was looking for. With the tweezers, he reached carefully toward the razor-sharp piece of torn metal on which the beef was speared.

He removed a bit, and examined it more closely.

It was flesh, a meaty chunk of what looked like reptile flesh.

Suddenly Nick had the creepy feeling he was being watched. Slipping the sample into the jar and fastening the lid, he turned quickly.

All he saw was Mendel a few feet away, snuffling back a sneeze as he ran his Geiger counter over the hull. And Elsie, on her knees, sifting through the sand at the base of the ship.

Then a flash of light from a bluff overlooking the beach caught his eye.

Squinting up at it, Nick saw the La Rochelle insurance investigators. They were loading their equipment into the back of a dark green van.

Their leader, the man called Phillipe, was standing behind the truck. He was staring down at the ship through a pair of binoculars. The binoculars were focused directly on Nick.

The Frenchman saw Nick looking up at him. Abruptly, he put away his field glasses and signaled to his men to hurry. Then he jumped into the van, and the moment the rear doors were slammed shut, he shouted to the driver, "*Allez*! Let's go!" The dark green van roared out of sight.

An hour later, Nick had forgotten the incident. He was airborne again, back in the giant military transport plane that had carried Colonel Hicks and the research team to Jamaica. Sitting on the floor of the plane, Nick was completely absorbed in studying the specimen he'd taken from the ship.

"Hey, be careful," he cautioned as a young soldier hurried past him with a computer printout for Colonel Hicks.

"Sir, we just got a report of three fishing boats, three trawlers, going down," the soldier called breathlessly.

Hicks looked up from the papers he was studying. "And?" he asked impatiently. "What does that have to do with us? What makes you think it's related?"

Elsie, who'd been reading her notes into her tape recorder, fell silent. Mendel stopped working on his calculator. Nick glanced up, too.

"The boats were *pulled* under, sir," the soldier said as Hicks grabbed the message and began reading through it. "Survivors report that there was something dragging on the underwater nets. Dragging so hard that the boats stopped moving. Then suddenly they were pulled underwater, backwards."

"All three of them?" Hicks crumpled the information sheet.

"Yes, sir. One at a time," the soldier confirmed, showing Hicks a map with X's indicating the area where the boats had gone down. "They weren't too far apart. The trawlers went under, one after the other."

Colonel Hicks spread out the map. "Okay, so what have we got?" He scanned the locations of the other episodes: the

Japanese fishing ship disaster off Polynesia, the demolished village in Panama, the torn, beached ship in Jamaica. "Traveling up from the sixty-seventh longitude to the forty-seventh parallel."

Elsie stood up abruptly. "Is that where the trawlers were sunk?" she asked, alarmed.

Hicks nodded, tracing the route with his finger. "Aw, no!" he rumbled. "Give me a break."

"It's off the East Coast, isn't it?" Mendel said.

"Two hundred miles off the American Eastern seaboard," Colonel Hicks said angrily. "And we don't even know what it is."

"*Theropoda allosaurus,*" Elsie announced.

They turned and stared at her. "It's a type of enormous reptile," she explained, "the likes of which died out in the Cretaceous period, we believe."

"So where has it been hiding for the last *sixty million years?*" Mendel Craven challenged, blowing his nose.

Elsie glared at him, and the scientist shrugged and timidly grinned back at her, fumbling with his tissues.

"But what about the traces of radiation?" Nick asked. "The radiation we registered in that fishing village in Panama and on the ship in Jamaica is not just some freak occurrence. It's the clue. With all due respect, Dr. Chapman," he told Elsie, "this thing, this creature, is far too large to be some lost dinosaur."

"Don't tell me what it's *not,*" Colonel Hicks barked, "I need to know what it is!"

"Okay." Nick attempted to sum up the facts. "What do we know? It was first sighted off the French Polynesian Pacific. An area that has been exposed to dozens of nuclear tests over the last thirty years."

"And you believe that's why we found radiation traces five thousand miles away?" Mendel said doubtfully.

"More than that," Nick hurried on, "I believe this is a mutated aberration, a hybrid caused by the fallout in that region."

"Say what?" Colonel Hicks said.

"Worm Man thinks we're looking at some mutant monster enjoying a nuclear growth spurt," Elsie said disparagingly.

"Like your giant earthworms?" Hicks asked.

"Yes," Nick said excitedly. "We're not looking at some archaic species that's suddenly reawakened after a billion-year snooze. We're seeing a never-before-known creature. The dawn of a new species. The first of its kind."

4

The old bum was carrying a beat-up fishing rod. Turning his greasy collar up against the rain, he shuffled past the loading docks and busy stalls of New York City's Fulton Fish Market.

The sidewalks were oily and glistening with scales. Not even the driving rain could wash away the stench of fish.

The bum stopped to rest under the FDR Drive.

"Gonna get yourself some lunch?" a man sitting on a filthy bare mattress, his back against one of the highway's girders, called out to him. "Gonna catch one of them delicious East River fish?"

In the shadowy darkness, several other men snickered and laughed.

"You never know," the old bum answered. "Sometimes you get lucky."

He left the shelter of the overpass and walked out onto the pier. At the farthest edge of the dock, he sat down and cast his line into the murky water.

Within seconds, the floating lure bobbed. The pole bent. The old man smiled to himself.

Suddenly the water began to churn. Something enormous started to rise out of the scummy river.

The old man's red-rimmed eyes bulged. He swallowed hard and scrambled to his feet as the huge back fins of a tremendous reptile burst from the river.

The bum dropped his rod and took off running. The dock behind him ripped apart as an awesome force lifted from beneath it.

Slipping and sliding in the rain, the bum skidded under the Drive. Shivering with fear, he hid behind a steel girder.

The creature rose, sending a tidal wave of water crashing down across the elevated highway, bending the steel girder like a paper clip.

A car washed over the guardrail. A yellow cab landed on top of it, crushing its hood. Screams erupted. The battered driver crawled out of the smashed taxi and was sucked into the river as the immense wave retreated.

Overhead, on the Drive, cars and trucks crashed and scraped against one another. Horns began to blare. People shrieked.

An enormous clawed foot with massive talons stepped over the highway, shattering the pavement.

Cars swerved to get out of its way. A boat tossed up from the river crashed down, severing the Drive. A van collided with the boat.

In one immense motion, an impossibly huge tail with a ridge of razor-sharp scales dragged across the Drive, sweeping the roadway clear of wreckage.

The earth shook as the creature moved inland toward the fish market.

Suddenly a cargo truck was lifted into the air, and a shower of crushed ice and hulking fish rained down on the street.

Sixty blocks away, midtown Manhattan was awash with rain.

"What a morning," Audrey muttered, ducking into the Athens Diner. She was soaked.

"I'll have a tuna on rye," she called. Brushing the rain off her brown leather jacket, she slid into the booth with Lucy and her husband, Victor "Animal" Palotti, WIDF's fearless roving news cameraman.

The Athens was bustling and noisy, its windows pleasantly fogged with steam. Above the counter, a television was tuned to WIDF's *News at Noon*. At least Caiman wasn't on, Audrey noted gratefully.

Across the table, Victor was digging into a cheeseburger and fries. A smear of ketchup clung to the cuff of his sweater. There was even a crumb dangling from the shock of dark hair that escaped from his backwards baseball cap.

It was easy to see how he got his nickname of Animal, Audrey thought, smiling at her best friend's hopelessly sloppy husband.

"Audrey, hey, how's it goin'?" he mumbled, flashing her a burger-filled smile.

"My life reeks," she replied.

"Oh, please." Lucy waved away the complaint. "Your life doesn't reek. *His* life reeks," she said, nodding across the table at Animal. "How can you eat like that?"

"Big bites," Animal quipped, shoveling some french fries into his already stuffed mouth.

"I can't believe Caiman was such a jerk. After everything I've done for him." Audrey took off her wet beret and tried to shake the rain off it. It had looked all fluffy and fashionable this morning. Now it resembled roadkill. "You know how I spent last weekend?" she said, stuffing the dead hat into her jacket pocket. "Walking his dog."

"The man is dirt," Lucy empathized, "Gutter slime, dog poo, puke chunks."

"Hey, hey, come on." Animal acted pained. "I'm eating here!"

Lucy rolled her eyes at him. "Yeah, right. Is that what you call it? Listen, Audrey," she said, turning to her friend, "you know what your problem is? You're too nice, that's your problem. You've got to be a killer to get ahead, you know what I'm saying?"

"That's not it," Audrey protested. "Animal, you don't think that's true, do you?"

"Nice guys finish last," said Animal, shrugging. "First rule of the jungle."

"Well, I can be tough if I want to," Audrey asserted.

Animal gave a barking laugh that sent a burst of french fries across the table.

"Sorry, baby," Lucy said, patting Audrey's hand sympathetically. "You haven't got that killer instinct. You just don't have what it takes."

"Oh my gosh!" Audrey shouted as the waitress delivered her sandwich.

"'Gosh'?" Lucy shook her head. "You see what I mean? Who says 'gosh'? Gosh is so *nice*."

"No, no, look!" Audrey grabbed the startled waitress's arm and pointed to the television set above the counter. "Turn it up. Turn that up," she urged. Releasing the woman, she hurried over to the counter and stared up at the TV.

PANAMA, read the green letters at the bottom of the screen. And there, walking alongside some military man on a pier, his raggedy knapsack strapped to his wide shoulders, his dark hair flopping over his eyes, in a sweatshirt and jeans, of course, was Nick.

"It's Nick!" Audrey hollered to Lucy. "My college sweetie,"

she said, not taking her eyes from the screen. "Look at him. He looks so handsome on TV. What's he doing in Panama?"

The weather report came on, and Audrey returned to the booth.

A short while later, when they were up at the cashier paying for their lunch, Lucy asked, "Did your college sweetie have a name?"

"Niko Tatopoulos," Audrey told her.

"Is that why you dumped him?" Animal teased.

"Very funny," Audrey replied. "No. I couldn't picture myself with someone who'd spend his summer picking apart cockroaches. It just seemed too boring."

Lucy laughed. "And now you live the glamorous life of Charles Caiman's assistant."

There was a dull thumping noise in the distance, as though an immense truck had hit a speed bump blocks away. Audrey felt the floor of the diner shudder, very faintly, beneath her feet.

She glanced out the steamy window. All she could see through the driving rain was the camera pole of the WIDF news van parked outside.

"How long were you and this guy going steady?" Animal asked, taking a toothpick from the dispenser on the counter.

"Nearly four years," Audrey confessed.

"Girl, I'm surprised he didn't ask you to marry him," Lucy said.

"That's the problem," Audrey explained. "He did."

Suddenly the distant thumping grew louder. This time, everyone in the diner seemed to notice it.

"Tell me that's not another lame parade," Lucy said.

The next thump rattled the dishes on the counter. Glasses

tumbled from a shelf behind the cashier. The toothpick dispenser fell to the floor.

"I don't think that's a parade," Animal said, whirling toward the window as another thump shook the entire building. Outside, people had begun to race through the rain.

An enormous dark shadow moved past the misty windows.

There was a screech of brakes outside, and then the unmistakable crunch of a car crash.

"Duck!" Animal yelled as a newspaper vending machine sailed directly into the front window, shattering it.

Then, suddenly, the diner was still.

"What was that?" Audrey whispered, gripping Lucy's arm. For once her friend was speechless.

"You don't want to know!" Animal assured her. "Get under the table! I've got to get this on tape."

"Victor, don't be stupid!" Lucy hollered. But he was halfway to the door.

Rain gusted into the diner through the broken window. Holding onto each other, Audrey and Lucy stared out at the destroyed street.

Water sprayed up from broken fire hydrants. Bricks and plaster fell from buildings. Cars were burning. The roof of Animal's news van had been crushed. The camera pole lay across the avenue like a fallen tree trunk.

Dodging falling debris, Animal ran to the truck.

"Don't!" Lucy shouted to him. "Please, please, Victor, come back."

He didn't hear her. He had pried open the bent back door of his van and was searching for his camera.

Lucy grabbed Audrey's hand. "We've got to stop him," she cried. They dashed through the shattered diner. By the time they got outside, Animal had grabbed his equipment and taken off running.

They saw him a moment before he reached the corner. He was racing full out, trying to jam a cassette into his video-cam.

"No!" Lucy screamed. "Come back here, Victor, you creep!"

But he swung around the corner and was gone.

Leaping over a crushed car door, Animal struggled to get the tape into his damaged camera. The thumping they'd heard inside the diner was overpoweringly loud out on the street. Animal glanced up. The air was filled with smoke and steam. Despite the rain, there were fires everywhere. Cars were burning, people screaming, scattering. A greenish-brown tower he had never noticed before was standing in the middle of the street.

Animal's jaw dropped as he scanned up the length of the tower.

It was . . . shaped like an enormous lizard. Its immense body was crusted with scales, its massive head ridged with spikes.

For a fraction of a second, Animal's mind raced to the giant helium balloons that sailed above the streets during the Macy's Thanksgiving Day parade. Anchored by sturdy ropes, the balloons took dozens of people to manage.

But the comparison was wishful thinking. Animal realized it instantly.

There was nothing hollow or helium-filled about this humongous beast. This lizard on steroids was solid, muscular, and pulsing with life.

Just then, the mammoth creature craned its thick neck. A fold of dense skin hung from its throat. Lifting its gigantic jaw, it bellowed into the sky.

The screaming in the streets grew frantic and piercing. Flocks of pigeons left the protection of building ledges and soared off in a dark cloud. Windows rattled. A huge pane of department store glass shattered. Its splintered shards crashed inches from Animal's back.

Though his heart was pounding and his hands had begun to shake, Animal forced the tape into his videocam.

Hoisting the machine onto his shoulder, he darted out into the middle of the street and began videotaping the wailing beast.

The camera moved slowly and deliberately upward. It took in every detail of the terrifying lizard until it reached the creature's howling head.

That head swung suddenly down. Yellow eyes bored into Animal through the camera lens. Then the lens went black.

Animal looked out from behind the camera to see what had happened.

He saw the underside of an immense foot poised above his head, ready to squash him like a bug.

Still shooting, the cameraman raced backwards as fast as he could.

The foot descended recklessly. Animal could not outrun it. Holding the camera over his head, one finger locked on the power button, he froze beneath the falling claw, paralyzed with fear.

The creature's foot slammed down.

The ground beneath Animal shook. Amazingly, he was not crushed. Not that he knew of, anyway. And he could see light, a sliver of light, above him.

Breathing hard, his chest heaving, Animal realized he was standing *between the lizard's toes*!

The gargantuan foot lifted abruptly. The street rumbled again as the terrifying giant continued his mystifying march.

Animal stared in amazement as an unbelievably immense tail swept past him. He was disoriented, lost for a moment as the huge lizard disappeared around a corner. Then he recognized what was left of an office building across the street. He realized where he was.

He was just a few blocks away from the studio. WIDF was practically around the corner — the same corner around which the gigantic lizard had just darted.

Animal blinked and checked his camera. The red light, the shooting light, was still on. "I got it," he murmured, amazed.

His heart was still pounding. His hands were trembling. The hatband of his backwards baseball cap was soaked with rain and sweat. Animal didn't care. He punched the sky with his fist. "I got it!" he yelled, grateful and terrified.

On the twelfth floor of the WIDF building, Charles Caiman paced before his office window. "I don't care!" the irate anchorman was shouting into the phone. "I don't give a rat's tail about some war in a rinky-dink country with a name I can't pronounce. Find me a decent story, will you?!"

The strange thumping noise had started up again. The building began to shake. "What is that?" Caiman demanded. "I can't hear myself think. Audrey, where are you? Where is she?!"

"She's at lunch now, Mr. Caiman," a young secretary told him.

The windows started to rattle. The lamp on Caiman's desk shook, its light flickering. The crisp color image on a nearby TV monitor turned suddenly snowy. Then the picture exploded. The screen went black.

At that moment, what looked like a massive green jaw

moved past the office window. A wet mouth opened. It was filled with huge, discolored teeth. And then a yellow eye came into view, an eye so immense it nearly filled the window.

The secretary began to shake and point.

"What?!" Caiman growled at the petrified girl.

"Er, I think your story just walked by the window," she said.

5

The military convoy sped along the New Jersey Turnpike. A jumbo jet banked low over the highway, heading for Newark Airport. The piercing scream of its engines failed to drown out the wail of sirens.

Fire engines, ambulances, and police cars zoomed in and out of traffic. Trucks and buses rumbled by. Cars honked. Helicopters thwacked overhead.

Home sweet home, Nick thought, yawning, as the Jeep he was riding in bounced wildly over a pothole. It had been three years since he'd been back to the States. It felt like almost that long since he'd gotten a decent night's sleep.

Every minute of the plane trip home had been spent checking data and exchanging theories with Elsie and Mendel. And then trying to figure out how the weird bulletins that kept interrupting them fit into the picture. The sunken fishing trawlers off the coast of Maine. The bizarre sightings of a sea monster near Cape Cod. And finally the extraordinary reports of a giant reptile wreaking havoc on Manhattan.

Even now, several miles across the river from the besieged

city, Nick could see scattered fires still burning. Plumes of smoke rose above the familiar New York skyline, darkening the overcast sky.

The convoy halted at the gate of a military camp. Colonel Hicks's car was up ahead. The driver showed his identification to the National Guardsman who had stopped them.

"Colonel. They're expecting you, sir." The guardsman saluted, and waved the line of trucks and Jeeps inside.

The camp was still in the process of being built. Bales of barbed wire were being rolled out around its borders. A dozen tents had been set up, and more were being raised. The base had been erected on a rocky ledge above a deserted strip of marshland on the New Jersey shore. It offered an awesome panorama of Manhattan.

Nick stared thoughtfully at the endangered island as the Jeeps pulled up in front of the main tent. Suddenly they were barraged by news crews.

"We've got nothing to say right now. No comment, no comment." Hicks spread his arms to shelter the scientists from the camera's glare. "Clear this bunch out," he ordered, plowing through the press and into the tent.

A young sergeant rushed over to greet them.

"Any word from the mayor's office?" Hicks demanded.

"Sergeant O'Neal, sir," the man introduced himself. "The mayor's office has agreed to evacuate the city. They've called out the National Guard."

"They're evacuating Manhattan?" Elsie said to Nick. "That's over three million people. Has that ever been done before?"

"I don't think so," Nick answered as Sergeant O'Neal led them through the command tent. It was still under construction. Equipment was being installed — generators and telephone lines, computers, radios, and TV monitors.

"Where is the creature?" Hicks asked, ignoring the chaos around them. "Where is he now?"

"We've lost sight of it, sir," the young sergeant answered crisply.

Hicks whirled on the man. "Excuse *me*? You want to run that by me again, son?"

O'Neal wilted. "After the initial attack," he said nervously, "it just . . . disappeared."

Nick noticed that the back of the command tent was open. He could see the city across the way. Military helicopters circled above it, scanning the wreckage.

"I don't understand," he mused, thinking. He walked over to O'Neal. "How can something that large just disappear?"

The sergeant shrugged uncomfortably. "We're not sure. We're checking the area now."

"He probably returned to the river," Elsie suggested.

Nick shook his head, studying the Manhattan skyline again. "I don't think so," he said, leading her to the opening at the rear of the tent. "I mean, it's an island, water on all sides. But look at those buildings." He gestured to the soaring skyscrapers. "That's a place where he can easily hide."

A soldier ran into the tent, nearly knocking them over. His face was flushed with excitement. "Channel Twelve caught it on film!" he shouted, running to the bank of video monitors that had just been installed. "Twelve," he told a technician who was adjusting the TVs. "Hurry up, turn it on."

The man switched on Channel 12. And there was Animal's video. The shaky picture was slightly blurred as the camera panned up the scaly swamp-green flesh of the creature's underbelly.

"WIDF's exclusive tape was taken less than a half hour ago," Charles Caiman's voice droned. The screen image cleared.

And there was the lizard's enormous head, the flap of pale skin dangling from his throat. The jaundiced eyes glared fiercely. The mouth, cavernous, filled with stained, spiked teeth, roared open.

Workers and military personnel had flocked to the tent to see the story. At the sight of that monstrous mouth, they stopped dead in their tracks.

"Cameraman Victor Palotti barely survived this vicious attack to provide us with this footage," Caiman's voice continued as the beast's immense foot came down around the cameraman.

Nick and Elsie exchanged stunned glances. "It's impossible. It's got to be some kind of hoax," Elsie murmured anxiously. "I mean, how tall is that building it was standing next to?"

Mendel pushed between them. "Maybe twenty stories high, thirty?"

"*Tall*," Nick said, remembering the giant footprints in the ruined village. "Still think it's a dinosaur, Dr. Chapman?"

Elsie shook her head. "It's too big."

"Ha," Mendel snorted. "That thing could trip over a dinosaur and not even notice."

"Please," Elsie Chapman whispered softly. "Please let it be a hoax."

The staff of WIDF was gathered around office monitors watching the same news story. As Animal's video ended, the room burst into applause. Everyone was yelling, "Way to go, Animal!" and "Okay, Victor!" and "That's our guy!"

"Great stuff, Animal." Audrey hugged the cameraman.

"Weren't you scared?" one of the news editors called out.

"Definitely." Animal tossed a couple of cassettes into the pocket of his lucky jacket. It was a long brown jacket, so old that the leather was cracked and flaking, but it had loads of pockets and compartments in which to stash film, battery packs, and camera lenses. "Sure I was scared. I thought Lucy was going to kill me," he joked.

Lucy punched him. "Yeah, and he was right," she told their coworkers with a laugh.

"People!" Murray, the station manager, entered the room and looked around anxiously. Packing crates and cartons were strewn everywhere. "Come on, come on!" Murray urged. "We have to be completely relocated to the New Jersey station before our ten o'clock broadcast."

The excitement and laughter faded as everyone turned back to the task of packing up the office. "Animal, you're in the chopper with Caiman." The station manager glanced at the TV monitor, then signaled to Animal. "He's just winding down. He'll be off in two seconds. Go on. They're up on the roof waiting for you."

Animal turned to Lucy. "You going to be all right?" he asked.

Her eyes instantly misted. But she stuck out her stubborn jaw and nodded. "Sure. I'm always all right. Anyway, Audrey's going to stay with us."

"You don't mind, do you?" Audrey asked him. "I can't stay in Manhattan. I mean, the whole city's being evacuated —"

"No problem," Animal assured her, then he bent to kiss Lucy goodbye.

"Better go," Lucy said, jerking her head at the monitor. "Ego Man is done."

Audrey glanced at the TV, too. Caiman was no longer on the air. Now one of WIDF's field reporters was updating the story from New Jersey. "Military and government health officials set up a command post on the New Jersey coast this afternoon," she was saying as the camera tracked a group of people scrambling out of Jeeps and heading purposefully through a crowd of waiting reporters.

And there was Nick again! Running a hand through his thick dark hair, with that big backpack slung over his shoulders, he was following this fierce guy in full uniform who kept waving the cameras away. Looking adorable and amazingly important, Nick Tatopoulos was hurrying into a tent on the command post in New Jersey.

"Audrey!" She whirled at the sound of Caiman's voice. He was rushing toward the elevator. "My bag?" he demanded, snapping his fingers at her.

Grabbing the briefcase, Audrey rushed through the chaotic office to him. "Mr. Caiman, I've got a lead," she announced, catching up with the anchorman. "I know a guy on the inside with the military."

"Not now." Caiman kept walking.

"You don't understand," she persisted, trotting alongside him. "I can get us some great background information —"

"No, *you* don't understand, honey," he cut her off, catching the elevator door as it was about to close. "This is the time when the big boys have to go to work, okay?" He stepped onto the crowded elevator and pointed at her hand. "The bag?"

Snatching Caiman's ID tag off his briefcase, Audrey threw the leather bag at him. The impact knocked him backwards as the doors closed.

For a moment, Audrey stared at the press pass in her hand. She couldn't believe what she'd done.

Then Lucy hollered, "Forget him. Get what you need and let's go!"

Outside, people were running in every direction.

Hundreds of New Yorkers were trying to leave the city at once. The streets were filled with people darting desperately around spewing hydrants, smoking building wreckage, and overturned cars.

Crowds of panicked pedestrians were trying to funnel into subway entrances.

Audrey and Lucy had no choice but to join them. In a mob of shouting, shoving commuters, they descended the subway stairs.

Audrey glanced up just in time to see the WIDF news helicopter lifting off the damaged building behind them. "There goes Animal!" she shouted to Lucy.

Three steps below, her friend looked up, but it was too late. The last glimpse of sky had given way to the grimy ceiling tiles of the subway station.

A television was turned on inside the token booth, its volume cranked up. Inching past the booth, Audrey could see an aerial view of the gridlocked city on the screen. And hear the unmistakably oily voice of Charles Caiman.

"Hundreds of thousands have jammed the streets in the largest evacuation in the history of the city," the anchorman was saying. "And many people are not happy about it."

"Now what makes him think that?" Lucy asked, rolling her eyes at Audrey over the bald head of the man wedged between them. "I'm happy. Are you happy?"

"What are we running from, anyway?" the bald man asked, with a look of disgust. "A big lizard? I've got cockroaches in my building that could wrestle that thing to the ground."

Four packed trains passed before they were able to push and wriggle their way onto a subway car. And then it was Cockroach Man who gave them the final neighborly shove aboard.

Minutes later, smashed together like sardines, Audrey carefully peeled the photograph off her WIDF employee ID card. Squished behind a schoolboy's bulky backpack, Lucy waited, holding Caiman's press pass.

"I don't know if this is a very good idea, Luce," Audrey said, handing the picture to her friend.

"What are you talking about?" Swaying back and forth in the cramped car, Lucy tried to place Audrey's photo over Caiman's. "You stole it. Finally you got up a little nerve. Don't wimp out on me now," she said.

"What if Caiman finds out?" Audrey asked.

"How often do you think you're going to have an ex-boyfriend on the inside of a major story? This is a once-in-a-lifetime chance. Give me some glue," Lucy demanded, clamping Audrey's photo to the press pass with her thumb.

"I left my forgery kit back at the office," Audrey informed her.

Lucy tapped the boy with the backpack. "Hey, kid," she said, "do you have any glue?"

"And what do I get?" the boy demanded.

Lucy glared at him. "The warm feeling of helping your fellow man," she growled.

The mayor of New York scrambled across the tarmac to his waiting helicopter. The beating blades set up a fierce wind. With one hand, the mayor ran his hand nervously through his thick white hair. With the other, he waved to the crowd of anxious businesspeople he had just tried to reassure.

One of them was racing after him. He was a rugged-looking guy with a bristly gray-black beard and tightly cropped dark hair. "Who is that jerk?" the mayor asked his aide.

"I don't know, but he could be a major campaign contributor," the aide reminded him.

The mayor smiled broadly as Phillipe hurried toward him.

"La Rochelle Insurance," Phillipe called in his thick French accent. He handed the mayor a business card. "We represent nearly thirteen percent of the buildings in your city."

"Nice to meet you, Mr. —" The mayor glanced at the card. "Roach, is it?"

"Roache," Phillipe shouted against the noise of the revolving blades. "It is pronounced Ro-shay."

"Yes, well." The mayor gestured to the waiting chopper. "I'm on my way to get an update from the military. Now, if you'll excuse me."

"Ah, certainly." Phillipe patted the mayor's back. "I just wanted to tell you that you can count on our support," he shouted, making certain the small device he'd planted on the mayor's collar was firmly in place.

"Thank you very much." The mayor shook Phillipe's hand, then turned away and sprinted up the steps into the helicopter. His aide shut the door behind him and the chopper lifted off. It climbed into a sky full of air traffic.

Police and news helicopters scanned the city. Others ferried military personnel across the river.

In the WIDF news helicopter, Caiman pulled off his mike and hollered to Animal, "Over there, that's the mayor's chopper."

"I thought the captain was supposed to go down with the ship," Animal said, training his camera on the silver craft with the Big Apple emblem.

"He's on his way to the briefing." They were banking toward the Jersey shore. "Is that it over there?" Caiman wanted to know, pointing at the acres of tents and trucks below them.

Animal nodded. "Must be."

Fifteen minutes later, they were at the base. Pushing through a gawking crowd, they ran through the rain to the media area. Two police officers stopped them.

"You need press ID past this point," one of the cops said.

"Don't you watch TV?" Caiman demanded.

The police exchanged looks. "Can we see your press pass, sir?" the second officer asked mildly.

Caiman reached automatically for the pass attached to his briefcase. It was missing. "I had one here on my bag," he told the cops, flustered. The anchorman searched his pockets, growing more agitated.

Finally, Animal showed his own ID to the officers. "He's with me," the cameraman assured the police, and together they plowed through the checkpoint.

6

Carrying a wet Yum Yum Doughnuts bag and a Styrofoam cup of coffee, Jean-Luc dashed across the street to the delivery van. The weather had been stormy all day. Now it was late afternoon and pouring again.

Down the road, past a row of deserted summer bungalows, the lanky Frenchman could see the lights of the military compound. Loops of razor wire gleamed in the rainy dusk.

Shifting the bag and cup, Jean-Luc pulled up his raincoat collar, then knocked on the back of the truck. Jean-Claude opened the rear doors and reached out a hand to help him up.

The inside of the old van was filled with state-of-the-art electronics gear. Phillipe had changed out of his business suit. In a black T-shirt and trousers, he paced behind two men and a woman who sat before the high-tech equipment, fiddling with the dials.

Jean-Luc set down the doughnuts and handed Phillipe the coffee. "Does it work?" he asked, unbelting his dripping raincoat.

"The idiot with *avoirdupois* is speaking now," Jean-Claude responded, reaching into the Yum Yum bag.

"The mayor?" Jean-Luc asked.

"*Oui*." Jean-Claude grinned. "He did not detect the device that Phillipe attached to his collar. Now he is our microphone."

Jean-Claude bit into the sugary doughnut and grimaced. "Bah!" He spat out the pastry. "No croissant?"

Phillipe took a sip of his coffee and winced. "What is this?" he demanded. "You call this coffee?"

Jean-Luc shrugged. "I call this America."

Setting down the Styrofoam cup, Phillipe reached over the shoulder of one of the seated men and turned up the volume. The mayor's voice came through perfectly.

"You're telling me that in an election month I've evacuated the entire city for nothing?!" they heard him rave.

"They are in the command tent?" Jean-Luc asked. Phillipe nodded.

"We've been monitoring the waters around the island," a new voice said.

Jean-Luc cocked his wet head at Jean-Claude. "That is the admiral," Jean-Claude explained, "Admiral Phelps."

"As far as we can tell it hasn't left the area," Phelps said.

"As far as you can tell?" It was the mayor again, annoyed. "Is that the best you people can come up with?"

"We think there's a strong reason to believe it may be hiding inside one of the buildings within the sequestered area." The men in the van recognized the strong, self-assured voice of Colonel Hicks.

"But you don't know for sure!" the mayor insisted.

There was a slight commotion in the tent, a rash of murmurs. Someone cleared his throat meaningfully.

"What is it?" Phillipe asked his engineers.

They shrugged. "An interruption," the woman said. "Perhaps someone has entered."

"One second, O'Neal," they heard Hicks say.

46

"Ah," said Phillipe, "you were right. It is the young sergeant. He has come in."

"Mr. Mayor," Hicks continued in a tight, controlled voice. "We cannot give the all-clear until we've checked each and every building! Now, if you'll excuse me for a moment. What is it, Sergeant O'Neal?"

"Well, sir, I . . ." O'Neal seemed reluctant to speak.

"Go on," Hicks prompted.

"Excuse me, sir, but doing a building-by-building search may be more difficult than we originally projected."

"More good news?!" the mayor snorted sarcastically.

The strangers in the delivery van leaned forward, straining to hear.

"What do you mean?" Hicks said.

"We've run into a problem," O'Neal said softly.

"So this is the city that never sleeps," Nick said, peering out of the speeding Jeep at devastated streets. Except for patrolling police and National Guard troops, and a handful of crazies and looters who had not yet left, Manhattan was eerily deserted.

"Let's hope that mutant lizard of yours is catching some Z's," Elsie Chapman said as the convoy Colonel Hicks had assembled raced downtown.

"Don't worry." Mendel sneezed, blew his nose, and blinked at Elsie. "I'll protect you."

She shot him a wilting look. "I appreciate the thought, Dr. Craven," she said crisply. "But I think our escorts are better qualified to handle the situation." Elsie indicated the truckful of soldiers in battle gear riding alongside their Jeep and the tank following it.

The convoy halted near the triangular Flatiron Building on

lower Broadway. Colonel Hicks and Sergeant O'Neal jumped out of the lead Jeep and raced across the avenue.

"Let's go," Hicks called to the scientists as he followed O'Neal all the way down the steps of the 23rd Street subway station.

By the time Nick sprinted around a capsized car, flashed his ID at the guard at the head of the stairs, and caught up with them, Sergeant O'Neal was standing at the edge of the train platform pointing something out to Colonel Hicks.

"Lieutenant Wells and his men found this late this afternoon." O'Neal gestured into the subway tunnel.

Hicks leaned over the platform to see it. Nick did, too. "Holy cow!" they heard Mendel wheeze behind them.

The four normal sets of tracks on which the local and express trains ran were twisted and mangled. And the four tunnels through which those tracks traveled were now, Nick saw, one jagged, gigantic cavern — a single tunnel enormous enough to hide a gargantuan creature.

Nick had been right. The creature was here, not out to sea.

Several soldiers with flashlights were moving cautiously toward the hole. A young soldier, Lieutentant Wells, Nick assumed, approached Hicks and O'Neal. "We were checking the office building above here when we discovered that the floor was gone."

Hicks looked up. Nick did, too. Not only was the ceiling above them missing, but the building had been hollowed out and torn to shreds.

The giant lizard had crashed through the walls of the office building from the street. Then he'd ripped up the floors and crawled down into the subway tunnels, burrowing through walls to carve out his cave.

"When we learned he could make his way through the tunnels, we realized he could be out of the quarantined zone," Sergeant O'Neal was explaining to Hicks.

"How many tunnels lead off the island?" Elsie broke in.

"Only five," Wells replied.

"We've checked them all," O'Neal added. "He hasn't used any of them."

"Have them sealed off," Colonel Hicks ordered

"And how should we do that, sir?" O'Neal asked.

"Fill them with cement," Hicks barked. "Brick them up, put land mines in them, bombs. I don't know. Just make sure that thing doesn't leave this island."

"Yes, sir." Lieutenant Wells jumped back onto the mangled tracks to join his men — a dozen soldiers armed with automatic weapons and flashlights, cautiously moving around inside a tunnel whose concrete walls and steel structural beams had been shattered by the immense reptile.

"You know, he's not an enemy trying to evade you," Nick said to Hicks and O'Neal. "He's just an animal."

"An animal? Did you see that thing on TV?" O'Neal shook his head. "We're not talking about some cat or dog here."

"What are you suggesting?" Hicks asked Nick.

"When I needed to catch earthworms —" he began.

"Earthworms?" O'Neal echoed in disbelief. "You've got to be kidding."

"Big earthworms," Hicks said. "Size of a dog or cat, right, Tatopoulos?" He exaggerated for effect.

O'Neal's eyes widened.

"Big earthworms," Nick acknowledged. "I knew the best way to catch them was not to dig them out, but draw them out."

"Lieutenant!" a voice from the tunnel called nervously. "There's stuff flopping around in here —"

"All we need to do," Nick continued, "is find out what it needs and he'll come to us."

"Like what?" Colonel Hicks wanted to know. "What could it need?"

"Fish!" the soldier in the tunnel shouted suddenly. "Lieutenant, there's fish stashed away in here. Whew. There's piles of them everywhere. Lots of fish."

Colonel Hicks looked at Nick. "Fish? Is that what we need to draw him out?"

"Looks like it," Nick agreed.

Four Apache helicopters banked over midtown Manhattan. "They're coming," one of the flyers radioed to Sergeant O'Neal.

Military technicians scrambled across the roof of the Flatiron Building, adjusting video camera cables. Down in the square, behind a sandbag barrier, O'Neal, in full battle gear, crouched in front of a blank monitor.

"There's twelve of them," the Apache radio operator continued. "Twelve big yellow dump trucks coming in over the bridge."

O'Neal acknowledged the report, then broke contact with the combat choppers.

From his vantage point, he could see his sharpshooters stationed on the rooftops and in the buildings surrounding Flatiron Square.

More units lay in wait behind barricades, benches, and trees in the small park across from the subway station.

A mobile rocket launcher was being hauled into place on the triangular traffic island where Fifth Avenue and Broadway cross.

*　　*　　*

In the command tent in New Jersey, Colonel Hicks was pacing before a wall of communications equipment. "What's going on? Are we set up or not?" he demanded.

"Delta Niner, what is convoy position?" a technician at the console radioed. "Colonel, sir, we've got guys over there putting the video cameras into place now."

"Good. Where are the trucks?"

"Command," a voice crackled over the radio, "they're just entering the city."

"This better work," Hicks said to his aide. "Can we get O'Neal?"

"We've got voice on him. No picture yet," the aide responded. "Any minute, though."

Just outside the tent, a burly blond repairman in blue overalls knelt next to a large satellite dish. The man attached a small device to a cable that snaked directly into the war room. He made a final adjustment, then tapped his earpiece and, in a French accent, spoke into his lapel. "It is good?"

Half a mile away, in a dingy motel room that had been transformed into a makeshift command center, a TV monitor came to life. The grainy picture it delivered was of Flatiron Square.

"Perfect," Phillipe said, pleased with the stolen video feed. "Jean-Claude, return to base."

At the same time, O'Neal's monitor blinked on, displaying a crisp color shot of the subway entrance. Then there was another aerial view, of the park this time. Then a long shot of Fifth Avenue came up, looking eerie and deserted, the trucks still out of range.

The rooftop video cameras had the area covered — the

buildings, the subway entrance, the park, and the traffic island. O'Neal could even see himself, kneeling behind the sandbags just in front of the Flatiron Building. And he could see a radio technician racing toward him.

"Estimated time of arrival for the convoy is five minutes, sir," the soldier reported breathlessly.

O'Neal checked the square. Darkness was falling fast. "Anyone seen Tatopoulos?" he asked. "He's hooked up, isn't he?"

Nodding, the radio operator handed O'Neal the mike. "Worm Man, do you read me?" O'Neal said. "Come in, Nick."

Sergeant O'Neal's voice crackled through the deserted subway station, where Nick was dropping coins into a vending machine. The sound startled him. He'd forgotten he was wired.

"Be right there," he hollered at the cracked vaulted ceiling of the station. "I forgot something." He pulled the lever and a disposable camera dropped from the slot.

"Let's go, Nick. Convoy ETA is five minutes."

Pocketing the camera, Nick leaned over the platform and stared into the long dark tunnel where the fish had been found. "You hungry, big guy?" he called. "Just hang in there. Dinner's on its way." Then he dashed up the subway steps.

He was standing alongside Sergeant O'Neal when a dozen huge yellow dump trucks pulled into the square. The smell was overpowering. O'Neal covered his nose with a handkerchief. "I sure hope your plan works," he muttered, squinting in the glare of the trucks' headlights.

"I'm kind of hoping the same thing," Nick confessed. With a racket of gears, the trucks began to unload their cargo. Tons and tons of fish tumbled to the street.

"Oh, man." O'Neal grimaced, amazed at the sight.

"That's a lot of fish," Nick agreed as a mountain of shiny-wet, flapping, squirming, iridescent blues and tuna, salmon and pike piled up in the center of Flatiron Square.

When the last of the trucks had unloaded and pulled out, O'Neal radioed all units to take their positions. Then he and his aides headed up to the rooftop command post overlooking the square.

Nick did not go with them. He remained near the sandbag barrier, where a couple of young officers were manning communications equipment. The video monitor beside them showed different aerial views of the sector.

Everything was ready.

Nothing was happening.

Five, then eight minutes passed. The lack of action and the total silence were unnerving. As were the skeptical looks the officers were aiming Nick's way.

Nick scanned the square. Something wasn't right. He'd missed something, but he couldn't quite nail down what it was.

There was steam pouring from a vent in the street. Glancing around, Nick saw several other vents sending up geysers of steam.

Borrowing a radio from one of the officers, he called O'Neal. "The subway vents," he said, urgently. "We have to shut them down. With the air pressure pushing up, he'll never smell the bait."

"Gotcha, Worm Man." Nick heard O'Neal issuing orders. Then the sergeant was back on the line. "Okay, we're on the case. Anything to send that stink down instead of up."

Moments later, with a loud whine, the vents shut down. The large whirling fan blades underground slowed to a stop. One by one the steam pillars billowing up from the street began to disappear.

The square seemed more silent than before, nervewrack-ingly still, as the waiting began again.

"No!" Nick's voice broke the silence.

He sprinted into the street, rushing toward a manhole cover only inches from the mountain of fish. Falling to his knees, he tried to remove the heavy steel cover. It was no use. It barely budged.

O'Neal saw him. "What now?" he radioed from the rooftop.

"We've got to open all the manholes!" Nick hollered. "The scent has to get down to him."

O'Neal gave the order, and Nick stepped back as soldiers rushed into the street to pull up the hefty disks covering the manholes.

They were almost finished when Nick glanced down a side street and spotted a cover in place.

Without thinking, he raced out of the square to the inter-section and tried to wrestle the steel hatch out of the gutter. Adrenaline fueling his effort, he grasped the cover and began to drag it clear.

Kneeling in the street, he heard the noise. It came up through the manhole from underground. There was a vibrating hum like the thunder of a low-flying jet. Like the first rumble of an earthquake, Nick thought.

He stared down into the dark hole, straining to see, to hear.

Half a block away, two parked cars jolted suddenly, banging against one another with an ugly crunch. Nick looked up.

The gutter beneath their wheels moved, hunched, buckled. Then the sidewalk split. An enormous crack splintered the pavement.

The crack traveled quickly along the street. It was heading directly for the manhole, directly for Nick.

Rattled, he scrambled to his feet, backing away from the hole.

The noise grew louder.

With a deafening roar, the ground erupted. The mammoth beast burst through, ripping up the street as he rose.

Nick ran. Debris showered down. A huge chunk of pavement fell in front of him, blocking his path. It was the piece of pavement on which he'd been standing only seconds ago, Nick realized, as the steel manhole cover he'd managed to remove rolled off the concrete fragment and clanged into a fire hydrant.

Panting, Nick turned. The immense lizard-like creature seemed to fill the street as he dragged himself up out of the ground.

Nick watched, frozen, awestruck. Fear and wonder gripped him equally. He could scarcely catch his breath as the massive reptile broke free of the pavement.

He was taller than the buildings around him. His huge head with its spiked crown craned up at the night sky. His neck was thick and roped with pulsing muscles. His chest, grained with glistening scales, heaved as he sniffed the air.

And then Nick noticed the mutant's tail. Ridged with a fringe of huge scales, it was nearly two stories high at its lowest point and seemed to go on for blocks.

Slowly, Nick pulled the disposable camera from his pocket and snapped a picture. The glare of the flashbulb caught the gigantic beast's attention. He spun toward the light. His colossal head swooped down, staring at Nick, almost eye to eye. A mist of dank breath soaked Nick's hair and beaded his face.

Suddenly the street was filled with soldiers. Guns trained, shoulder-hoisted rocket launchers prepared, they surrounded the giant lizard. But the sight of the incredible creature paralyzed them. They, too, could only stare up at him in shock and amazement.

Out of the corner of his eye, Nick saw the troops. Gently, he signaled with his hands for them not to fire. The beast, whose yellow eyes were disturbingly alert, blinked. Sensing somehow that the danger had passed, it lifted its fearsome head again, stepped over Nick, and moved toward the scent of fish.

The encounter had occurred on a side street. The rooftop cameras hadn't caught it. They'd only recorded the frantic movement of men and weapons. "What's going on down there?" O'Neal asked.

Just then, the lizard's massive head moved by, inches from O'Neal's. Everyone on the roof stared in silent shock, overwhelmed by the enormous creature as he walked past them, heading for the square.

They watched, riveted, until the beast's monstrous tail whipped by overhead. It smashed two of the rooftop video cameras, barely missing the startled soldiers as they dived for cover.

In the street below, excited and amazed, Nick rushed to catch up with the mammoth reptile, who had reached the pile of fish. As the creature feasted, soldiers stood and gaped, their weapons idle in their hands.

Miles across the river, Colonel Hicks and his staff watched the monitors stunned and astonished at the sight of the towering creature. Elsie, the mayor, and everyone in the tent stood frozen before the screen. Finally Hicks grabbed the radio. "Fire at will!" he ordered.

O'Neal delivered the message to his awestruck troops. "Fire! Now! Fire at will! Do it!" The soldiers snapped out of their stupor. From every corner of the square, they took aim and fired.

"No!" Nick shouted. "Wait!"

His words were drowned in a firestorm of bullets.

The humongous creature reared up screaming. Wheeling abruptly, his immense tail swept a dozen armed men from the street, tossing them against walls and windows with devastating force.

Three sidewinder missiles were fired from the mobile launcher in the park. Their screeching sound alerted the beast. He ducked and the lethal projectiles slammed into the building behind him, exploding on impact.

Bricks and glass rained down onto the square. Video cameras toppled, blowing up as they hit the street. Nick ran for cover. As he raced across Broadway, a large bronze statue toppled off its pedestal, trapping him, unharmed, beneath it. He stared out at the street and saw a battalion of tanks moving toward the square.

Barely able to roll onto his back, Nick turned to see the creature directly in their line of fire. "Watch out," he muttered. "Run."

Just then the mutant lizard spun around, racing at the tanks. With stunning swiftness, he bulldozed through them, squashing several beneath his huge claws.

In New Jersey, Colonel Hicks stared at a bank of monitors that showed only static or devastation. The mayor paced behind him, demanding an explanation. "O'Neal," Hicks radioed, "what's going on there?!"

"He's gone, sir," O'Neal responded. "Our command post was hit by friendly fire. We're out of action. Echo division is in pursuit."

Monster mash! It was hard enough to get a cab in New York before Godzilla came to town!

"I'm singing in the mud, just scooping up my worms...."
Dr. Nick Tatopoulos worked for the U.S. Nuclear Regulatory
Commission. He studied the effects of radiation on
earthworms. He liked his work.

"What did you see, old man?" Phillipe Roache coaxed the terrified
Japanese sailor who had seen Godzilla. Phillipe worked for the
French Secret Service. He, too, liked his work.

"Think I should ask him?" Audrey Timmonds, an assistant at WIDF, a New York City TV station, asked Lucy Palotti. Audrey wanted a promotion, but was nervous about approaching her boss.

Charles Caiman the name you trust in news

"I need to know this job is going someplace," Audrey told Charles Caiman. But her pompous boss did not take her seriously.

"Guess who's coming to town?" The titanic lizard, ferocious and agile, has arrived in New York!

"We fed him," Nick noted as Godzilla devoured truckloads of fish and then escaped.

"*He's* pregnant?" Nick tested his theory scientifically and came up with positive results!

"Just be calm, don't startle them." Good advice from Animal to Audrey as hundreds of hungry Baby Godzillas hatched at once, ready to take over the world!

In a tense moment, Nick came face-to-face with Godzilla!

Godzilla might not have been the most gracious guest New York has ever hosted. But he did leave a lovely parting gift.

"Your missiles hit the Flatiron Building?" the mayor demanded angrily.

Hicks ignored him. "Get me Echo division," he ordered, turning to his map table. "They should be just below Times Square. What have they got, four armored vehicles?"

"Six," an aide answered.

"What's our air cover in the area?" Hicks wanted to know.

"I'll check it out. We've got reports of looting in midtown," the aide added, "and it looks like that's where the thing is heading."

"Echo division is on the line." The communications officer handed the radio to Hicks.

"Echo division. Any sight of him?" the colonel asked.

"He's kind of hard to miss, sir." The voice of the division's radio officer was shaky. "We've got five armored vehicles left. They're chasing him now. He's fast, Colonel Hicks, sir."

"Fire at him," Hicks snapped. "That'll slow him down."

"Hasn't so far," the officer reported. "But we're in pursuit. Oh, no! He just creamed our lead vehicle. Stepped on it."

"He stepped on a tank?" The mayor tried to wrestle the radio mike away from Colonel Hicks. "Where is he? If he's in Times Square," the mayor ranted into the microphone, "keep him away from Forty-second Street. The city put up a fortune to overhaul the area."

"Yeah, well, tell that to the looters," came the response. "They're tearing up the place. Two guys are lugging a pinball machine out of the All Star Cafe right now —"

Suddenly a series of deafening thuds resounded through the speakers.

"What's that noise?" the mayor asked, wide-eyed.

"It's him," Elsie decided after a moment. "He's running. You're listening to about a hundred tons of reptile sprinting."

Hicks pulled the mike away from the mayor. "I want all civilians out of that sector. Clear that area fast!" he shouted.

There was a shattering crash of metal. "It's cleared," said Echo division's operator. "He stomped on the pickup."

"What pickup?" Hicks demanded.

"The one the guys were trying to shove that pinball machine into — uh-oh, he just stubbed his toe on one of our tanks. Flipped it over."

Hicks winced at the sound of the overturned armored vehicle sliding ferociously, slamming into obstacles, and, finally, he winced at the sound of splintering glass.

In less than a second, a strange new noise resounded through the speakers — a tornado-like wind, a howling gale of air followed by metal skidding through the streets.

"What is that?" Hicks demanded.

"You won't believe it." The communications officer at the scene choked back a sob. "He was hiding, sir. He disappeared around a corner and when our vehicles gave chase, he blew them away."

"With what? Don't tell me that thing is armed," Hicks demanded.

"With his breath, sir," the distraught radio operator tried to explain. "When our AVs turned the corner, he was waiting for them. He blew them away. Literally."

"Holy cow." Mendel Craven whistled. "He plans, he strategizes!"

"We've got nothing left here, sir. Nothing more to throw at

him," the operator continued. "He's heading east. We've got nothing capable of giving chase."

"Order in an air strike. Now!" Hicks shouted to one of his aides. "Where are our Apache helicopters?"

Moments later, four combat helicopters swooped down over the city. "We have him," the lead pilot radioed back to command. "He's moving east at a good clip, but we've got him locked on."

Hicks looked at a three-dimensional electronic grid of the city. The Apaches, four red blips on the screen, were speeding crosstown, tracking the mutant. "Then fire!" Hicks ordered.

It was not that simple.

The gargantuan reptile glanced up as a person might when sensing flies buzzing near. He stopped for a second, staring at the swiftly descending choppers.

The helicopters came screaming down on him, firing rockets.

With what seemed like a sigh, a blast of breath that rattled the attacking Apaches, the creature wheeled abruptly and disappeared around a corner.

The rockets blasted into the Chrysler Building. Shards of glass rained down as the landmark structure crumbled. The crowned dome of the famous building crashed into the street.

"Did you get him?" Hicks shouted.

The helicopter pilot's voice came through, filtered by heavy static. "That is a negative impact," he said.

"Negative impact!?!" It was the mayor. "It's the Chrysler Building!" he screamed. "Your people are destroying my city!"

"What happened?" Hicks demanded. "I thought you said he was locked on!"

The helicopters zoomed around the corner in pursuit. "Sir,"

the pilot responded, slowing his craft and maneuvering cautiously through the narrow side street, "the heat seekers can't lock. He's colder than the buildings around him."

All four helicopters had slowed and were carefully scanning the area.

The lead pilot spotted it first. An enormous hole had been torn into an old factory building on the south side of the street. He pointed down at it. "He's got to be in there," he radioed.

The others nodded, then opened fire, destroying what was left of the building.

An anguished scream echoed through the narrow street. It seemed to come from the smoldering remains of the demolished factory. The Apache pilots stopped firing and stared into the smoking wreckage. "I think we got him," one of them said.

He was wrong.

With a bloodcurdling roar, the monster exploded from a building behind them.

His gale-force breath battered the choppers, twisting the blades of the one nearest to him. It crashed into a building, then plunged to earth. The colossal jaws caught another one in mid-fall and clapped shut, crushing it.

The monster whirled, clawing a third ship out of the air. The swatted helicopter slammed into the ground. Again, as quickly as he had appeared, he vanished.

Colonel Hicks was on his feet, steaming mad. "Apache Two," he was shouting into the radio, "where is he?!"

The last of the pilots swerved around. "I don't know, sir. He just disappeared," he reported, shaken. The lone pilot proceeded cautiously along the empty street, scanning the remaining buildings.

He flew past a towering windowless structure, a dingy

gray storage facility of some sort. As he passed the building, the pilot caught a movement out of the corner of his eye. A shape shifted. Looking over his shoulder, he gasped, "Oh, no," realizing too late that, like a chameleon, the giant lizard had taken on the color of the building and hidden against it.

The pilot gunned his chopper, full throttle. Even at top speed, it could not outrun the immense creature. With a swipe of his enormous claw, the beast swatted the last Apache out of the sky.

Sergeant O'Neal and several of his men lifted the statue off Nick. The young scientist scrambled to his feet and surveyed the damage around him.

The square was a disaster. Mangled military vehicles and equipment littered the street. A tree lay across the road where a tank had plowed into it. Video cameras were smashed, cable lines torn up.

Building bricks, glass, and mortar, the rubble of the futile missile attack, lay scattered among the few fish the creature had been forced to leave behind when the firing began.

"You all right?" O'Neal asked.

"I'm fine." Then, Nick noticed something on the ground. He knelt down to get a closer look. It was a large reddish-brown puddle of blood. Nick knew it was Godzilla's He quickly scooped up a sample and put it in a small glass container.

"I can't believe it," the military man was saying. "He did all this, and basically, we did nothing to him."

"That's not true," Nick assured O'Neal. "We fed him."

8

The media had overrun the small city where the command post was set up. Mobile broadcasting vans with their satellite dishes were double-parked on both sides of the main street leading to the camp. News crews milled behind a security fence outside the briefing tent. Positioned so that the big tent loomed impressively behind them, network anchors were taping their stories.

Audrey pushed her way through the crowd, trying to stay out of the blinding lights aimed at the on-camera reporters. As she passed them, she could hear snippets of the night's news.

"Rumors continue to mount as to the origin of this, perhaps, lost dinosaur," a woman with flawless blond hair announced, staring earnestly into the camera. "How's my blouse?" she asked her cameraman suddenly. "Are you getting glare?"

Audrey touched the press credentials pinned to her own blouse. The glue had definitely dried on the picture of herself that she and Lucy had pasted over Caiman's smug face. Patting the forged pass, she elbowed past a camera crew taping a rival network's anchorperson.

"The President today declared a state of emergency," the athletic-looking newsman reported, "and has issued disaster relief funds to New York City —"

Audrey was almost at the command tent when she froze in her tracks.

"Maintaining a total media blackout, officials remain silent this evening as to their progress in containing this creature," she heard Charles Caiman declare.

Ducking behind two strangers, she peeked out at the squat newsman. The spotlight on Caiman was too bright for him to focus on anything but Animal's camera. Neither of them had seen her.

Relieved, Audrey hurried away, hoping to lose herself in the crowd.

Abruptly, the crowd shifted.

A line of military vehicles was approaching the compound. Suddenly everyone was rushing to meet it. Jostling and shoving, news crews surged toward the entrance gates, carrying Audrey along with them.

With the swarming media blocking its path, the convoy couldn't get into the command area. Stalled on the main street, in the fourth car back, Nick peered out at the pandemonium.

Over the heads of the advancing crowd, he noticed a pharmacy. Hesitating for a moment, he glanced at the blood sample, then made up his mind. "It's okay, I'll get out here," he told the driver.

The street was clogged with people. In addition to the crush of TV and print reporters, vendors selling dinosaur toys and balloons had set up shop on the road to the compound command center.

Copies of the now-famous WIDF news video were stacked

in cardboard trays next to T-shirts with images of the huge lizard taken from that same clip.

Nick hurried through the chaos toward the drugstore that he had seen.

That was when Audrey spotted him. Through the dense crowd moving her forward, she saw him in the distance. He was wearing an old bomber jacket and the same canvas backpack he'd carried in that news story from Panama.

"Nick!" she called excitedly, waving at him. But, of course, between the press shouting out questions to the returning military men and the vendors hawking their merchandise, he couldn't hear her.

Nick hurried into the drugstore.

"Do you have any home pregnancy tests?" he asked the pharmacist. "Especially ones that test for gonadotropic hormones or clomiphene citrate?"

"Let's see," the druggist said, gathering a handful of packages from the shelf behind him. "I think these six are about what we've got."

"I'll take them all." Nick pulled out his wallet and paid for the tests while the pharmacist put the six boxes into a paper bag.

"Nick?" a voice behind him asked.

Nick turned.

"Audrey?" he said, startled.

A huge unrestrained smile lit his face. She looked taller than he remembered, and skinnier, and her wild hair was longer than she used to wear it, but just as curly and blond. And the way she was dressed, all . . . well, sophisticated, he guessed. He could hardly believe his eyes, but it was Audrey. Beautiful, blond Audrey Timmonds.

"Is that really you?" he asked stupidly. He knew the grin was dumb, but there was nothing he could do about it. He felt ridiculous. And sounded worse. "Hi, hello. You look, wow, uh, how've you been?"

At least she was smiling, too. "It's good to see you, Nick," she said as the pharmacist handed him the bag and his change. He scooped up the money and they walked out together.

"So, you made it," he said, back on the crowded sidewalk.

"What?" she asked.

He pointed to the forged ID card she was wearing, not realizing, of course, that it *was* forged. "You're a reporter. That's what you always wanted to be, right? Hey," he said, feeling his grin finally fade. "I'm happy for you."

"Yeah, well," Audrey said dismissively.

"No, really. I am," Nick insisted.

"You still picking apart cockroaches?" she asked.

"I'm into earthworms now," he said, with just a hint of coolness. "But, hey, I wouldn't want to *bore* you with my work."

"You're still mad at me."

"Well, you left me without a phone call, a letter, nothing. All this time. Yeah," Nick said. "I guess I am still a little mad."

"That was years ago," she said defensively. "Some people change, you know."

"Most people don't," he said sharply.

Tears stung her eyes. She took a deep breath and drew herself up. "I'm sorry you feel that way," she said with as much dignity as she could muster. Then she turned and started to walk away. She had no idea where she was going. Certainly not back to that zoo outside the command tent to listen to Caiman taping the story of the century.

"Audrey," she heard Nick call after her. "Wait. You're right," he said when she turned. "It's been a long time. How about . . . Can I offer you a cup of tea?"

"Sure," she said, with an embarrassing rush of relief. "I'd like that."

It was not exactly like old times. They'd grown up and grown apart, of course. But the small private tent in which Nick had just set up a minilab did remind her of his messy, book-strewn room off campus where they'd laughed and argued and studied together.

"I still can't believe it," Audrey said now as Nick ripped open the boxes he'd bought and began to mix some of the contents together. "How does a guy go from being an anti-nuke activist to working for the Nuclear Regulatory Commission?"

"When we used to go to rallies in college, it was to help create awareness," he reminded her, taking his metal case from the floor and setting it onto the improvised lab table. "But from the inside now, I can actually effect change." Nick couldn't help himself. With a small, self-satisfied smile, he added, "*I* never lost my idealism." Then he snapped open the case.

And there on the inside lid were photographs of her, dozens of pictures from long ago when they were young and in love. She was surprised that Nick still kept them, and unexpectedly touched. Audrey cleared her throat. "So exactly what kind of changes are you trying to effect?"

He carefully took a beaker from his equipment case. "I'm preparing a census for the government, cataloging new species that have been created as a direct result of nuclear contamination," he explained, while pouring his mixture into the beaker.

"Nuclear contamination?" Audrey was suddenly alert. "Is

that what you think caused this creature? You think it's a new species, some mutant creature caused by toxic waste or acid rain or nuclear fallout or something?"

"Yes," Nick said, "I think it was probably nuclear fallout. I found this blood sample earlier tonight —"

"Blood sample?" She was surprised. "How close did you get to it?"

Nick shrugged. "Pretty close," he said, and laughed.

Audrey laughed, too. It felt good to be with him, comfortable and familiar. "What else did you find out?"

Nick finished his concoction, then added the blood sample to it. He took the piece of litmus paper from one of the test boxes and dipped it into the mix.

"Well, we know he eats tons of fish," he replied, glancing at his watch. "And that he's of the reptile genus. Obviously, he's a burrower. He's amphibious, and —" He pulled out the litmus paper and examined it. "And . . . he's pregnant!"

"*He* is?" Audrey said, confused.

Excited, Nick began to gather his materials together. "Obviously these tests weren't designed for this. But basically they're looking for the same hormonal patterns —"

"I don't get it," Audrey interrupted. "You said new species. If it's the first of its kind, how can it be pregnant? Doesn't it need a mate?"

"Not all species do. I bet he's one of those." Nick began to pace excitedly. "I kept wondering why he would travel all this way. But it makes perfect sense. All kinds of creatures have been known to go great distances for reproduction. That's why he came to New York. He's nesting!"

"Nesting?" Audrey echoed.

"Yes. Do you realize that a lizard can lay as many as a dozen eggs at a time? Think about it." Gathering up the beaker and his blood sample, Nick moved to the door of the tent. "Audrey, I'm sorry, but I've got to get this into the lab right away. To confirm all this. I'll be right back, okay?"

"Sure," she said. "Go on."

He rushed out and she sat on his cot for a minute, then got up and began to poke around. She opened his metal case again and looked at the old pictures of them together. She flipped through a book. It was dull stuff, full of graphs and charts.

There was a television set in the corner. She walked over to it and noticed a videotape labeled *First Sighting* sitting on the VCR. Unable to resist, she popped the cassette into the machine and turned on the TV.

What she saw was a wrinkled old Japanese man rocking back and forth on a hospital bed. Someone was asking him questions. But the man kept repeating only one word, "Gojira," over and over.

Audrey hit fast-forward. The tape whirred ahead to an aerial view of enormous footprints tracking through a jungle. She fast-forwarded the tape again and this time saw a massive ship stranded on a beach. Its side had been torn in a peculiar pattern, as if huge claws had ripped through the steel hull.

Her heart began to pound. Had she stumbled onto a top-secret video that showed the damage that the mutant lizard had wreaked around the world? What a story, what an exclusive for her! What had that old man in the hospital bed said? "Gojira," Audrey whispered, echoing the terrified cook's cry.

She rewound the tape and stared at the blank screen for a moment, conflicted about what to do. It was Nick's cassette. She could wait until he came back and . . . what? Ask him for it? Tell him she was desperate to become what he already thought she was, a real reporter?

You've got to be a killer to get ahead, she could practically hear Lucy urging her. *Nice guys finish last*, Animal had advised.

Audrey popped out the tape and stuck it into her purse. She glanced quickly around the tent. Should she leave Nick a note? The voices came at her again. *What are you, nuts?* they said. *What's your note going to say? "Stole your tape, catch you later"?*

There was a great clap of thunder outside. Rain began to drum on the roof of the tent. Audrey peeked outside, then took off running.

The WIDF news van was parked just outside the compound gates. She dashed toward it through the downpour, hoping that the computers in the truck were hooked up. She had some research to do. And she had to find Animal.

He was inside the van, shooting the breeze with Ed Mullins, one of the editors.

"Great!" Audrey cried, shaking the rain out of her hair. "Just the guys I need. Can you hang for ten minutes? I've got some major footage for a segment I want you to shoot and edit. But first I've got to write the piece."

"Sure," Ed said. "Who's going to do it?"

"I am," she defiantly announced, rushing to the computer. "I'll explain later. You guys don't speak Japanese, do you?"

"Sure," Animal said. "Sushi. Honda. Sony. Tofutti —"

It was morning when they finished taping. Locked inside the editing bay, they watched the segment on two monitors.

"Which is why," Audrey's voice came through the speakers, "in this case 'all the king's horses and all the king's men' may not be able to put the Big Apple together again. Audrey Timmonds, WIDF."

72

"That's it," Ed said, flipping off the picture. "You owe me a breakfast."

Animal was leaning against the editing console. "It's a real good piece, Aud. How'd you get hold of the material?"

She thought of Nick and winced. "I . . . borrowed it from a friend."

"Is he with the CIA? Or should I say, *was* he?" Animal grinned. "That footage looked classified. Must be some good friend to risk a career for you."

"You think he'll get in trouble?" Audrey blurted.

Animal shrugged his shoulders. "If he really gave you that cassette —"

"Well, he didn't actually, you know, like, hand it to me, so probably he'll be okay. Anyway, weren't you the one who said, 'Nice guys finish last'?"

Ed handed her the cassette and she hugged him. Rushing out of the truck into the dawn drizzle, she saw Murray, the station manager, standing next to Caiman. The anchorman was about to do a live spot with another cameraman.

She tugged at Murray's WIDF team jacket. "Murray, I've got exclusive footage," she whispered, while Caiman shouted that the rain was ruining his hair and streaking his makeup and were they ready yet. "I've got a video of other places this thing has attacked."

Murray was suddenly interested. "Shoot him. Shoot him now," he cued the cameraman. "You do?" he asked Audrey. "Whose story is it?"

"Mine," she announced.

Daylight filtered through the blinds in the musty motel room a half mile from the compound. Jean-Claude's high-powered binoculars were trained on a small tent a few yards

73

from the command tent. "The one they call Worm Man is leaving his tent," the blond agent announced. "He is running to the briefing."

"And the girl has not returned?" At a desk nearby, Phillipe stroked his short, peppery stubble and rifled through the photographs spread out before him. "I do not see her picture. Do we know who she is?"

"Not yet," Jean-Claude continued. "Ah, he has entered the command tent. They are all there now."

"We are ready," Jean-Luc called from the radio console. He flicked on the speakers and Colonel Hicks's voice filled the dusty room.

"That's all we know about it," Hicks was saying irritably. "Next question."

"There he is." Jean-Luc pointed carefully at the monitor. "Dr. Tatopoulos. Taking a seat beside the Chapman woman."

The command tent was filled with VIPs. The mayor sat behind the governor, who was leaning forward, whispering something to a Presidential aide sitting a row in front of him. Other seats were occupied by congressional and military brass. Off to one side, grasping folders full of data, sat the science team.

"Colonel Hicks," an Air Force colonel called out, "what makes you believe another attempt to gun that thing down will work?"

Hicks forced a gracious smile. "If we lure him out into a more open area" — he walked over to a large map of Manhattan — "such as this portion of Central Park," he said, pointing to the poster, "we should be able to take him down."

"Take him down?" The mayor stood suddenly. "Last time you didn't even scratch him!"

"That's not true," Hicks exclaimed heatedly. "Our worm

guy —" He gestured at Nick. "Er, I mean, Dr. Tatopoulos found blood."

Nick stopped arranging his papers and smiled weakly as all eyes turned to him. "Yes, I did," he confirmed.

"You see." Hicks was tapping the map again. "All we need to do is lure him into more open terrain and get weapons that don't rely on heat seeking."

Nick raised his hand. "Excuse me, sir, but the situation's more complicated than that —"

"Nick, not now," Elsie cautioned him. Mendel merely rolled his eyes.

"What are you talking about?" Hicks asked.

Nick said, "Well, the blood I recovered revealed that the creature is either about to lay eggs or already has."

There was a barrage of questions, and then the governor stood up. "Are you trying to tell us there's *another* one of those things out there?" he demanded.

"I don't believe so," Nick responded.

"Then how can it be pregnant?" the mayor shouted.

"It reproduces without a mate," Mendel explained. "At least, that's what we think. Isn't that right, Nick?" he added, trying to ignore Elsie's angry frown.

"Yes," Nick said. "That's why we have to find the nest. If we don't, dozens more will be born, each one capable of laying eggs on its own. Very quickly, we could be looking at an enormous population."

"No problem." Colonel Hicks tried to calm his agitated audience. "After we kill the creature, we'll search for the nest."

Nick glanced at Elsie. She shook her head. "They don't get it," she told him. "I knew they wouldn't. Go on, as long as you've spilled the beans. Give them the bad news."

"It may be too late by then," Nick informed Hicks. "These eggs will hatch very quickly."

"How could you possibly know that?" Hicks asked.

"The fish," Nick told him. "The fish we found down in the subway, Colonel Hicks. He's not gathering all that food for himself. He's preparing to feed his young."

Suddenly everyone was calling out at once. Elsie shut her eyes. "I knew this would happen," she muttered underneath her breath.

"Okay, okay! Let's everyone settle down!" Hicks was yelling.

An aide entered the tent and whispered something into the governor's ear. The governor nodded his approval.

"If Dr. Tatopoulos is right," Sergeant O'Neal called over the hectic questions and expressions of concern, "we've got to act quickly before this problem escalates."

A general with a chestful of medals stood abruptly. "You want to divide our efforts based solely on some wild theory? I say blast the creature with all we've got. We don't have personnel to spare for a . . . an egg hunt!"

"General Anderson," Hicks replied with deference. "With all due respect, sir, Nick's come through for us before and if he feels strongly —"

"Came through for you!?" the old warrior stormed. "Colonel, your campaign's a disaster. You weren't even able to prevent this thing from coming to Manhattan."

"Gentlemen, excuse me." The governor stepped between them. "I've just been informed of something I think will be of interest to us all." He signaled to his aide, who hurried to the television and turned it on. "I think we should see this."

All eyes turned toward the TV monitor. And there was the

76

footage of the old Japanese cook, rocking back and forth on his hospital bed.

"What's he saying?" someone called out.

The image of the terror-stricken seaman froze and Charles Caiman's face replaced it. "From an old Japanese sailor's song called *Godzilla*," Caiman announced in his persuasive baritone, "a mythological sea dragon who attacked sailors, to our own modern-day terror. Who is this Godzilla, where did he come from, and why is he here? Tune in to my special report tonight. . . ."

"Godzilla?" The strange name was murmured throughout the command tent.

"What is this?" Hicks demanded.

"An ad for tonight's WIDF news special," the governor's aide said.

". . . A path can be traced back from Manhattan all the way back to the French Polynesians, where nuclear testing has been going on for over twenty years," Caiman was saying in his report.

General Anderson glared at Hicks. Hicks felt his normally controlled face burn with embarrassment.

"Research team member Dr. Niko Padoplus," the newscaster continued in his irritating, pompous way, "believes the creature is nesting, using Manhattan as ground zero to cultivate his species . . ."

Anderson turned on Nick. "You went to the press with this?!" the general accused.

"No," Nick stammered, "I didn't . . . I didn't talk with any-one."

"They mentioned you by name!" Anderson roared.

"Yes . . . but I . . ." Nick had no idea what had happened. He hadn't given the cassette to anyone. It was still in his tent, he was sure. In his tent, where he had left Audrey . . . who, for some reason, had left without saying goodbye, without a note. Which seemed to be a habit of hers.

"You gave them the tape?" Colonel Hicks thundered.

"No, it's still in my . . . tent," he said weakly as a possibility began to dawn on him. "It's . . ." Nick shut his eyes and shook his head. "She took it," he muttered.

Furious, General Anderson stalked across the briefing room and stopped inches from Nick. "Pack your stuff. You're officially off this project. As of now," he commanded.

Across the street from the base, where Audrey and Animal had been eating lunch, the television was also tuned to WIDF. The trio stared transfixed at the countertop monitor playing Caiman's promo.

". . . and in this reporter's opinion," the pompous anchorman announced, "'all the king's horses and all the king's men . . .'"

"It's *Gojira*, you moron!" Audrey jumped up. "And that is not *your* report. It's mine!" she yelled at the TV. "He stole my report! That's *my* story! I'm the one who found that stupid song!"

"Don't miss my exclusive tapes of Godzilla's worldwide terror spree." Caiman's ad spot was winding down. "Tune in tonight for my special report on *Godzilla*!"

Audrey wadded up her napkin and heaved it at the TV. "Caiman, you reek!" she shouted.

A few blocks away, Phillipe snapped off the TV monitor in his motel room. "Idiots," he declared. "It is bad enough they call their doughnuts 'croissants' and their undrinkable coffee 'French roast'! Now they are calling the beast 'Godzilla'!"

"They fired Tatopoulos," Jean-Claude said.

Phillipe walked over to the window and stared out through the blinds, thinking. Then he turned abruptly. "Pack up," he ordered. "We're leaving."

9

In the phone booth outside the restaurant, Audrey was trying to reach Murray. She'd been trying since ten-thirty, just after the first teaser for "Caiman's exclusive" had appeared. It was almost noon now. "What do you mean he's not there?" she barked to the station manager's secretary. "A second ago you told me he was on the other line."

She was put on hold again. Through the downpour she could see the entrance to the compound. A taxicab had just pulled up outside the gates and was waiting for someone. She thought of Nick and winced. He was in there somewhere. She only hoped he hadn't seen that dumb teaser yet.

Godzilla! That mini-moron Caiman couldn't even get the name right. And now that was what everyone was calling the nuclear mutant. She'd heard it a dozen times already this morning — in the restaurant, and out here on the street.

A couple of minutes ago, two kids had run past the phone booth, making threatening claws of their hands and screaming, "Godzilla's going to get you!" And what had she done? Audrey shook her head, recalling the moment. She'd leaned out of the booth like a crazy woman and yelled at them, "It's *Gojira!*"

Animal had seen her and burst out laughing. He was waiting

inside the diner, in a window booth, watching her. Audrey clicked the receiver a couple of times. "Murray, you coward," she said, "get on the phone. At least have the guts to talk to me."

Probably Animal was right. Probably Caiman, the nationally known anchorman, had pulled rank on Murray, a lowly station manager, and threatened to have him fired or something. What a jerk Caiman was. What a sneaky, rotten jerk.

And what a jerk she had been, Audrey thought, her anger giving way to the misery of guilt and regret. She only hoped that Nick, being Nick, was so wrapped up in his work that he hadn't had time to watch TV. There was a chance he hadn't seen the promo piece. If only she could get to him before he did. . . .

Her eyes shifted back to the military camp gates. Someone was coming out. It was a civilian, a guy with a backpack, lugging a couple of suitcases. One of them was metal just like the case Nick kept his equipment in, the one with the old pictures of them together.

It *was* Nick! He was heading for the waiting cab. Audrey hung up and ran out into the rain.

"Where to?" the cabbie asked as Nick opened the rear door.

"Newark Airport," he responded glumly.

Audrey came up behind him. "You're leaving. Why?" He glanced at her, then turned away and continued to load his bags into the cab. "It's because of me, right? Because of the story?"

"What did you think was going to happen?" he said.

"You never said it was off the record," she answered lamely.

"I shouldn't have to, Audrey," he shot back at her. "You're supposed to be my friend."

Animal had seen Audrey dash out of the phone booth. He'd quickly stuffed half a blueberry muffin into his mouth, gulped down the last of his coffee, and run outside to find out what was up. Now he waited a few feet away near his news van. Huddled under a tree trying to stay dry, he heard Audrey say, "I didn't mean for it to turn out like this."

"Right," Nick answered coldly.

"Look, I lied to you," she continued. Her hair was soaked and plastered to her head, and she was squinting against the rain. "I'm not a reporter," she confessed. "Nick, when we broke up and I came out to New York, I was so sure I'd make it. But I haven't. That's why I needed this story so badly. I just couldn't tell you I'm a failure."

"So you thought that made it okay to steal my tape?"

"No," Audrey said. "That was a terrible thing to do. I never should have done that."

Nick hurled his backpack into the cab and climbed in after it. "Good luck in your new career. I really think you have what it takes," he said, and slammed the door. The cab lurched off.

"I'm sorry," Audrey said softly.

From under the flimsy shelter of the tree, Animal watched her. She was just standing there in the rain, staring after the taxi. He took a step toward her, then suddenly changed his mind. Instead, he jumped into his van and roared off after the cab — which, he was surprised to see, was driving right past the turnpike entrance.

Animal had assumed the taxi was going to the airport. Well, he thought now, maybe he'd been wrong. Or maybe the driver knew a shortcut.

Inside the cab, Nick noticed the mistake, too. "Excuse me," he said, "aren't we going to the airport? I don't think this is the way."

The cabbie ignored him. They were driving down a long empty street near the waterfront. There was a series of warehouses up ahead. Nick tapped on the glass partition. "Hello. Excuse me, where do you think you're going?" Again there was no answer. The driver never even turned his head.

"Do you speak English?" Nick asked more insistently. He was beginning to get nervous. "Let me out here," he yelled, reaching for the door. Before he could grab the handle, there was an ominous *click*. The doors locked.

"All right, stop the car, right now!" Nick shouted.

To his surprise, the cab stopped.

"Good." He cleared his throat in the uncomfortable silence. "Now let me out."

The driver turned to face him. His tightly cropped salt-and-pepper hair and craggy face seemed strangely familiar. He slid open the glass partition. "I am afraid I cannot do that," the cabbie said in heavily accented English.

"Hey, I know you, don't I?" Nick asked, eyeing him suspiciously.

"I don't think so," the driver insisted.

"Yes," Nick remembered. "You're that insurance guy."

"I am Agent Phillipe Roache," the bearded man confessed. He pulled out a badge and opened it for Nick to see. "Of the SDECE. The French Secret Service. Your American friends are not going to look for the nest."

"Are you sure?" Nick asked, alarmed. "How do you know?"

"We know," Phillipe said. "Trust me."

"Trust you! You hijacked me," Nick reminded him. "Now you want me to trust you? And why would I do that?"

"Because, Dr. Tatopoulos," the French secret agent replied, "you are the only one who wants to find the nest as much as I do."

Phillipe drove around to the loading dock of a seemingly deserted warehouse. A garage door opened and the cab pulled inside.

"What is this?" Nick asked, amazed. The immense building

was filled with equipment. Radios, guns, explosives, even Jeeps, trucks, and fully armored tanks lined the space. Phillipe's men were everywhere, setting up monitors, loading boxes onto trucks, and repainting vehicles to resemble those of the U.S. Army.

A number of the men looked up as Nick and Phillipe got out of the cab. A few of them looked familiar to Nick. They seemed to recognize him, too. Some nodded in greeting, a few smiled. Phillipe introduced them, then gave Nick a quick tour.

"How did you get all this stuff into the country?" Nick asked, flabbergasted at the military hardware piled up around them.

"This is America," Phillipe replied. "There is nothing you cannot buy."

"Except a decent cup of coffee," Jean-Claude interjected. He was at the communications console, where Phillipe had paused to examine a written report.

"So why all the secrecy?" Nick asked. "Why aren't you guys working *with* the U.S. military?"

"I am not permitted to speak of such things," Phillipe declared.

"You said you wanted my trust," Nick said sharply. "Then I need yours."

Phillipe glared at Jean-Claude, who had involuntarily chuckled at the exchange. The blond agent shrugged without apologizing. "Very well," said Phillipe, turning to Nick. "Try to understand. I am a patriot. I love my counry. Can you understand that?"

"Sure," Nick conceded.

"It is my job to protect my country. Sometimes I must even protect it from itself, from mistakes we have made. Mistakes that we do not want the world to know about."

Nick understood. "You're talking about the nuclear testing in the Pacific."

"Yes," Phillipe confessed. "This testing done by my country left a terrible mess."

"The radioactive fallout," Nick said.

Phillipe nodded. "I believe the fallout infected some of the area's species and helped to create . . ." He paused, searching for the right word.

"Godzilla," Jean-Claude finished the sentence.

"This dangerous situation," Phillipe said, ignoring him. "We are here to clean it up."

An hour later, they were bent over the map table, studying a grid of Manhattan.

Unbeknownst to them, Animal was outside, soaked to the skin and trying not to slip off the garbage Dumpster. He'd been perched on the narrow edge of the trash bin for twenty minutes, peering into the warehouse through the narrow slit of a window that had been cracked open for air. His hands ached from gripping the sill. He wasn't sure how much longer he could hang on, but what he'd seen so far was worth every cold, wet, knuckle-busting minute of pain.

"They will set the trap at eight-thirty," he heard Jean-Claude call from the radio console.

Phillipe acknowledged the message with a curt nod. "We know how to get into the city," he was telling Nick. "We just do not know where to start looking."

Nick moved closer to the map, then put his finger on the Flatiron Square area. "Here," he said. "The subway station at Twenty-third Street. Where we first found the fish. With a little luck, this will lead us right to him."

"Us?" Phillipe said, smiling. "So you're in?"

"I'm in," Nick affirmed. "I always wanted to join the French Foreign Legion."

It was midafternoon by the time Animal got home. He raced up the stairs and took out his keys. The apartment door opened before he had a chance to use them. He was staring at some guy he'd never seen before.

"Who are you?" Animal demanded.

"Arthur." The man put out his hand. "You must be another refugee from Manhattan. Come on in. If you have nowhere else to stay, stay with Lucy and Victor."

"I *am* Victor!" Animal snarled, pushing past the guy and into an apartment filled with strangers. Lucy was passing among them, pouring coffee. "Excuse me, who are these people?"

"What?!" Lucy said defensively. "I couldn't just let them sleep in the street. They were forced out of their apartments because of Godzilla. They've got nowhere to go."

"Where's Audrey?" Animal asked, kissing the upturned cheek Lucy offered him.

"In the bedroom. Crying her eyes out because of you," she said. "All that 'you gotta be vicious' stuff you filled her head with."

"You were the one —" Animal began.

"Go in there." Lucy shoved him gently toward the back bedroom. "Talk to her."

Audrey was sitting cross-legged on the bed, crumpled tissues piled up all around her. She was staring through tear-swollen eyes at the TV, watching a press conference in progress.

Someone identified on the screen as General D. K. Anderson was saying, "Contrary to some very irresponsible reporting, we have no information to lead us to believe that any eggs of this creature exist."

"It's all my fault," Audrey wailed suddenly "What have I done, Animal? What have I become? Look at me. This isn't me. I don't do things like this."

"We all make mistakes, Audrey," he tried to console her.

"Yeah, well, I just totally messed up with the only man who ever really cared about me," she protested.

"Maybe not," Animal said carefully. "If you could make it all up to him, would you?"

"Of course I would!" She blew into a fresh tissue, then tossed it onto the pile.

"Good. Listen up. I followed him after he left you. I was going to try to talk some sense into the jerk when all of a sudden the guy pulls into this warehouse filled with a bunch of French wackos who want to try to sneak into the city tonight."

"Is he crazy?" Audrey said.

"You tell me."

She thought for a moment, trying to make sense of it. "They're going after the nest," she exclaimed.

"Exactly. And if he finds it," Animal said, "you should be the one to show the world that he was right all along."

Audrey stared at him. Suddenly she understood. Her eyes widened. "You want me to follow him into the city?"

Animal went to the closet and pulled a big overcoat from the rack. "We both will," he said, slipping the coat on over his damp camera jacket. "It'll be fun." He started going through drawers, taking out a flashlight, battery packs, and blank video-tapes, and stuffing them into the pockets of both the coat and the beat-up old jacket.

"I don't know," Audrey said. "I've already made such a mess of things."

Animal walked over to the window. "Audrey, I'm going after them. You can come with me or not." He opened the bedroom window and began to climb out.

"What are you doing?" Audrey jumped up and grabbed her coat.

"I can't leave by the front door," the fearless cameraman confessed. "Lucy'll kill me if she finds out."

They were dressed in U.S. combat uniforms, Nick, Phillipe, and all of the men in the warehouse. As they prepared to board their vehicles, Phillipe handed each of them a stick of chewing gum. "What's that for?" Nick asked, climbing into the passenger seat of a repainted truck.

"It will make us look more American." Phillipe got behind the wheel.

Nick rolled his eyes. "You'd better let me do all the talking," he decided as the convoy pulled out into the rainy twilight.

They made their way to the New Jersey side of the Lincoln Tunnel. A line of military trucks and tanks was passing through a guarded blockade. Military police were checking each vehicle before it was allowed to enter the tunnel to Manhattan. Phillipe's convoy slipped into line behind the last of the trucks.

"Who you boys with?" A guard with a clipboard walked up to their window.

"Oh." Nick leaned past Phillipe and improvised wildly. "We're with the Three-Two."

"I didn't ask you, soldier," the guard snapped.

"Sergeant O'Neal just called down for us to join them, sir," he tried again, indicating the military vehicles moving into the tunnel ahead of them.

The guard glared at Nick, then looked Phillipe over suspiciously. "You got a problem talkin'?" he challenged.

"Wah, no sir," Phillipe answered in a perfect Southern accent. "Ah'm fine."

The MP didn't look convinced, but the trucks behind Phillipe's began honking impatiently and he waved them through. "Okay, keep it moving."

"Thank you verrah much," Phillipe drawled. Nick was stunned. "I love Elvis movies," Phillipe explained as they entered the tunnel. "He was the King!"

10

"What is this place?" Audrey asked.

They were standing in front of a door set in the base of an abandoned overpass. Through shoulder-high weeds, she could see a military roadblock that was keeping traffic backed up for miles, and beyond that, across the river, the skyline of Manhattan.

"It's a vent to the Hudson tubes, the subway tunnel," Animal said, prying a rusty padlock off the old iron door. "It should take us directly into the city, to the Twenty-third Street station."

"You've got to be kidding," Audrey said. "There are rats down there."

"Rats, mice, roaches, and one large lizard." Animal pulled open the creaking door and, before she could protest, led her through the musty darkness and down a ladder onto the tracks.

They followed the tracks through the train tunnel, Animal's flashlight leading the way. "Watch your step around here," he cautioned as the flashlight's beam picked out a land mine.

"What is that?" she asked.

"They've booby-trapped the tunnels so our friend Godzilla can't use them," he explained, stepping over the mine and cautiously walking on.

Audrey swallowed hard and followed.

Across the Hudson, Phillipe's assault team had reached Flatiron Square.

"They have prepared his dinner," Jean-Claude reported as the men raced down the steps of the 23rd Street subway station. He was listening in on a conversation between Colonel Hicks and Sergeant O'Neal. "O'Neal says they are ready. The meadow in Central Park is filled with fish. They have tanks, rockets, and soldiers ringing the area. They are waiting for Godzilla to 'come and get it.'"

"If Nick is correct, he will leave the nest soon. Ready?" Phillipe turned to Nick.

"Let's do it," Nick said. Hopping off the platform ledge, he led Phillipe's men past an abandoned subway car, into the huge cave the beast had hollowed out.

A dozen flashlight beams crisscrossed over the rough earth floor of the subway, following a trail of dead fish. The decaying remains marked the path of the mammoth lizard. Near the platform they'd spotted only a few dead fish. But as Phillipe's men moved cautiously deeper into the tunnel, there were more, many more.

The more fish they saw, the closer they were to Godzilla's nest. And the fierce mutant, Nick knew, would defend that nest to the death.

Suddenly the faint humming sound in the subway stopped. Everyone froze as the wind shifted direction. The stench of fish filled the tunnel.

92

"They've turned off the ventilation system," Nick explained. "They're calling him to dinner."

"Let's hope we are not the hors d'oeuvres," Phillipe said.

Half a mile behind them, Animal kicked in a broken steel door and burst onto the platform. His video camera was perched on his shoulder, ready to roll.

Audrey followed him. Stepping delicately over the carcass of a large fish, she shone her flashlight across the wall of the ruined station. "Twenty-third Street," she read. "I can't believe we made it."

Looking through his camera lens, Animal saw beams of light moving deep in the tunnel. "They're in there," he whispered. "Let's go." Scrambling down from the platform, he took off after Nick and his team.

"Are you sure it's them?" Audrey asked weakly. But Animal was already running along the broken rails toward the now-faint lights. Squeamishly, she lowered herself onto the tracks and followed him.

The air grew stifling and foul the closer they got to the huge tunnel. The smell of ripe fish was overwhelming. A subway car, its cracked windows etched with graffiti, was sidetracked at the entrance. "Can you see them?" Audrey called to Animal, who was several feet ahead of her. "Is it Nick?"

Suddenly Animal stopped short. The ground started to quake. Dust fell from the ceiling. "Oh, no," Audrey whispered, frozen with fear.

Half a mile ahead, Nick was kneeling down, searching through his backpack for a new battery, when the tremor hit. He looked up quickly, as did the rest of the assault team.

A terrible screeching sound erupted in the distance.

Nick clambered to his feet as the earth trembled again. Phillipe's men stopped in their tracks. "Godzilla," one of them whispered.

The screeching grew louder. The tunnel shook with thumping footfalls. Pipes clanged and debris rained down.

Suddenly a wall collapsed.

The colossal beast burst through it.

Massive claws burrowing, he blasted his way into the huge cave, moving with awesome speed toward the men.

The team scattered. Most of them dived into a huge sewer pipe, which rolled and shook as the fierce creature shot past, narrowly missing them. The tunnel quaked beneath his humongous strides.

Audrey and Animal were a few yards inside the tunnel entrance. "Animal, let's get out of here," she begged, tugging at his oversized coat. But he'd started filming and wasn't about to stop now.

The entire station was shaking. "Animal, please! Hurry! Let's go!" Audrey yelled. Finally, with concrete falling all around them, he started moving backwards.

Trying to keep their balance against the shifting earth, they made it out of the tunnel. A moment later, the mammoth beast was inches behind them.

They dove out of his way, into the broken subway car. Crawling desperately along the wildly rocking floor, Audrey pulled herself toward a window. She peeked out, just in time to see the amazingly muscular creature crawling up and out through the station ceiling. It was a breathtaking sight. He moved so quickly and effortlessly for such an enormous thing.

"Are you getting this on tape? Tape it!" she whispered to Animal. Although she was shaken and scared and sickened by the odors and cold darkness, Audrey realized that she was watching the giant reptile with a crazy kind of admiration.

It wasn't his fault, she found herself thinking. He wasn't trying to kill anyone. If Nick was right, the creature only wanted to gather food for its young.

Animal had caught the last moments of the gargantuan lizard's climb. The beast was gone now. Dark sky showed through the immense hole he'd left. Rain began to drum on the roof of the subway car. Audrey and Animal stood up. And then, with relief, they began to laugh.

Inside the tunnel, Nick and the assault team emerged from the pipe. Nick stared for a moment at the jagged new hole the reptile had ripped in the wall. "I guess we go this way," he said.

"While he dines, we find the nest, no?" Phillipe said, following him. "How much time do you think we will have?"

"If they kill him," Jean-Claude said, "we have all the time in the world."

"Not really." Nick led them through the new passageway. "Whether he returns or not, those eggs will hatch," he explained, "and probably soon. He must have come from the nest. If we can trace his path backwards, we'll find it."

"What if he returns while we are there?" It was Jean-Luc who spoke this time. He shrugged his thin shoulders. "He is clever. Maybe he will sense their trap and return at once."

"Jean-Claude," Phillipe ordered, "find out what is happening!"

The brawny French agent switched on his radio and listened through headphones as they followed the route the creature had taken.

It was pitch-black in the new tunnel, and wet. Their flashlight beams showed a wide underground alleyway littered with broken train tracks. Rotten fish floated in inches of sewer water.

Moving as quickly as possible, they splashed through the sludge. Phillipe glanced at his compass. "We are moving northwest," he said.

One of his men, a young soldier named Pierre, pulled out a map of the city and, holding it under his flashlight, showed it to Phillipe.

"Nick," Phillipe called, "if we continue in this direction, look!" He traced the route with his finger. It led to Penn Station, a huge commuter railway station.

Nick whistled. "I hope you're wrong," he said. "From there tunnels and tracks lead all over the Northeast."

"Wait," Jean-Claude said when they had sloshed through the rank water for a while. "They have seen him! A team of spotters on a rooftop on Central Park South is reporting to O'Neal now." He switched on the speakers. The team stopped and gathered around the radio.

"Target's heading north to section five," they heard. And then, with the filtered thumping of the creature's footsteps in the background, another voice excitedly reported, "He's moving up Seventh Avenue. Okay, he's here. He's at the perimeter of the park, sir, at Central Park South."

The voice grew suddenly secretive, breathless with fear and disbelief. "Oh, no. He just looked at me. I can see his face. He's taller than this building. He sees the lights on the field. Something's wrong, sir. He's glaring at them. It's almost like he knows."

O'Neal's voice came through the static. "He's staying within the shelter of the buildings. Move, move. Come on, big guy," he urged. "Give us a shot at you." Then he ordered, "Don't fire until he's cleared the buildings and moved into the park."

"Let's go," Nick said. Jean-Claude shouldered the radio receiver, and they hurried on.

The assault team rounded another bend. "Over there." Phillipe's flashlight found the end of the vast tunnel.

Nick put on a burst of speed, sprinting out into an immense space. The men followed. A dozen flashlight beams quickly took stock of the building they had entered, crisscrossing the huge area.

The structure had been torn to shreds. Scattered fish were everywhere. It was clear that they had found Godzilla's den.

"You were right," Nick said, stunned. "We're in Penn Station — or what's left of it."

High above, there was a gigantic hole in the tall ceiling. "What is it?" Phillipe asked. "What is up there?"

But Nick's flashlight was focused on an object directly under the hole. It was a huge sign that had crashed down from above. Electric sparks were still dancing off the dangling wires. MADISON SQUARE GARDEN, the sign read.

"Unbelievable!" Nick gasped. "It's the scoreboard. That hole above us opens into Madison Square Garden. It's New York's most famous sports arena," he explained. "That big broken box on the floor is the scoreboard!"

"He got away!" Jean-Claude called suddenly. "The fools fired too soon. He took one step into the park and someone issued the order to fire. But he turned and ran. They are chasing him now, shooting at him. They have called in the Apache helicopters."

"Now he will return, no?" It was Jean-Luc. In the darkness, they could hear him rapidly assembling his automatic weapon.

"I don't think so," Nick responded. "He'll have to lose them first. He won't take a chance on leading them to his nest."

"You believe he is so clever?" Phillipe asked.

"You've seen him?" Nick said.

"Only the pictures." Phillipe thought about it, then he nodded. "I think you are right. We must hurry."

Helicopters zoomed down the canyon of Seventh Avenue, firing wildly.

The immense beast roared, swatting furiously at the attacking missiles. Two of them whistled past his head, exploding the buildings behind him.

From the surrounding rooftops, sharpshooters were ripping up everything around him.

He whirled abruptly. His mighty tail whipped across the tops of several buildings, sending soldiers and equipment crashing to the street. A penthouse terrace, torn from the front of a luxury high-rise, fell forty stories, flattening two assault vehicles.

A chunk of metal from one of the squashed tanks flew wildly, spiraling into the park. It landed next to O'Neal, who was crouched at the radio, trying to hear what Colonel Hicks was saying above the deafening din of the battle.

"Shoot it!" Hicks shouted from the command center. "Fire, O'Neal. Give him everything we've got. Just don't let him get away!"

O'Neal looked through his field glasses. Godzilla was moving with amazing speed, dodging a volley of rocket fire. O'Neal could see the mammoth head above the buildings, spittle dripping from its bellowing jaws.

The Apaches streaked after him, but the beast was too quick. He turned his head abruptly. His thick tongue flicked out and caught two helicopters.

With a snap of his iron jaws, he swallowed one and cut the other in two. The remains of the severed chopper smashed into a church steeple, knocking it over with a clamor of bells.

The massive creature continued racing west. Suddenly O'Neal realized what was happening. "He's heading for the river!" he hollered to Hicks.

A minute later, a tidal wave of water rose up from the Hudson River, crashing down on the West Side piers and parking lots. Cars and trucks washed inland, crashing through the streets like bowling pins. "It's too late," the stunned sergeant reported. "He's gone."

"Don't worry." Hicks's voice crackled through the receiver. "Admiral Phelps has a little something waiting for him."

Beneath the murky waters of the Hudson River were three nuclear submarines, the *Indiana,* the *Anchorage,* and the *Utah.*

"We've got him on sonar," the captain of the *Utah* radioed as a large mass appeared suddenly on the ship's screen.

Alarms sounded on the *Indiana.* "He's on the grid. We're closing in," the second sub reported.

"That thing is moving fast," the *Anchorage*'s radio operator announced. "Sonar's blipping like crazy."

"Get him locked on," Admiral Phelps commanded. Hicks was standing beside him in the command tent, checking the progress of the ships and their target on a three-dimensional computer grid.

"What's he doing?" the *Utah*'s operator called in suddenly. "He's coming right at us —"

On his computer screen, Hicks watched the mass speeding toward the lead sub. "Tell them to fire!" he ordered Phelps.

"We're locked on," the *Indiana* radioed.

"Fire!" Phelps hollered. "Fire at will!"

The *Indiana* obeyed. The torpedo shot out, darting directly at the underwater mass.

The creature swerved abruptly. But Hicks could see the torpedo turning, too. He watched it tracking the great beast. Then, with phenomenal suddenness, the target began to dive.

"Where'd he go?" the *Anchorage*'s captain demanded.

By the time Hicks knew, it was too late. The gigantic beast had dived under the *Anchorage*, then shot upwards, ramming the huge sub. The entire ship spun. Twisting over onto its side, it collided directly with the torpedo.

An enormous spray of water erupted from the river, and bubbles and debris floated to the surface. On the computer screen in the command tent, the *Anchorage* vanished.

"We've lost him, sir." The *Indiana*'s radio operator sounded dazed.

Colonel Hicks watched the screen. "Phelps!" he shouted. "He's shifted course. He's heading back toward Manhattan."

"The *Utah*'s closing in," the admiral said. He lifted the mike. "Close in and lock on, *Utah*," he ordered. "*Indiana*, lock him on. Fire before he makes land again!"

Hicks was already on the the radio to Sergeant O'Neal. "Deploy troops along the waterfront. He's moving toward the city. I want him stopped this time! If he sets even one of those big ugly toes on land, blast him with everything we've got! Do you read me, Sergeant?!"

"Yes, sir," O'Neal replied.

Boxed in by the subs, the powerful beast plowed toward the shoreline of Manhattan and began burrowing furiously into a sewer pipe. As his huge claws dug, bursts of dirt clouded the waters around him.

"Impact in eight seconds," an ensign on the *Utah* reported. "Seven, six . . ."

"Target locked on, sir," the *Indiana* confirmed. "Missiles launched."

There was a chilling silence in the command center.

Hicks and Admiral Phelps stared at the computer screen. "Five, four, three, two . . ." they heard.

The lethal torpedoes sailed toward their target, disappearing into the undersea dust cloud surrounding the great beast. An enormous explosion burst from its center, sending shock waves booming through the water.

On the shore, O'Neal's forces were waiting with more firepower than had ever been thrown at the mutant before.

Suddenly, from the river, a towering geyser blew high into the air. Debris shot up from the murky bottom waters. Wreckage rained down on the troops. A huge raw chunk of scaly flesh landed less than a yard from O'Neal. It could have been the remains of an enormous fish. Or, O'Neal hoped, his ears still ringing with the blast, it was all that was left of Godzilla.

"Direct hit!" the *Utah* reported.

"We got him!" Admiral Phelps hollered as the blip that had been the beast disappeared from the computer screen.

11

Audrey and Animal moved cautiously through what was left of Penn Station. Their flashlights played across the fish-littered ruins.

"Oh, man, no," Animal grumbled as they discovered the fallen scoreboard. "Don't tell me that big freak wiped out Madison Square Garden, too. No more Knicks games. No more Rangers."

Audrey stared up at the hole in the station's ceiling. "Is that it, up there?"

"That's the Garden," Animal confirmed.

"You think that's where his nest is?" Audrey was whispering. There was something in the air, besides the overpowering stench of fish, that told her they were in the creature's domain.

A sharp noise overhead startled them. Animal raised his flashlight toward the torn dome of the station. "I don't know about the nest," he said, "but something's moving around up there."

"Now what?" Audrey asked.

He pointed to a length of heavy cable dangling from the hole in the ceiling. "We climb," he said.

Madison Square Garden had been gutted. It was pitch-black. Jean-Luc had found the main circuit board and was trying to get the electricity working again. Until then, only dim flashlight beams lit the destroyed arena.

Nick, Phillipe, and the others picked their way through the mess. Seats had been torn out. Fish lay strewn everywhere. In some places they were piled up more than a foot deep.

It was hard to walk. And very dangerous. There were holes in the floor that went all the way down, not just into the huge plaza of Penn Station, but even below that, to the dark torn-up train tracks and platforms underground.

In a black corner of the trashed auditorium, Nick's flashlight picked out a strange clump of tall oval objects. Cautiously, he moved closer to it. Phillipe followed.

"Eggs," Nick said softly. They stared in disbelief at a pile of strange-looking reptile eggs — each one nearly twice as tall as they were.

Phillipe circled the heap. The beam of his flashlight lit one of the eggs from behind, making it appear almost transparent.

Inside the egg, something was moving.

"Only three." Nick surveyed the towering clump. "I thought there would be more."

"You were right." A few feet away, Jean-Claude's voice was filled with wonder.

Nick turned to the awestruck French agent. He was staring, open-jawed, at dozens of eggs lit by the assault team's flashlights.

Nick whistled softy, impressed. "There's got to be over twenty eggs."

At that moment, Jean-Luc threw the main switch. The arena was suddenly flooded with light. The team faced a stunning scene. Hundreds of the huge eggs were clumped inside the cavernous space.

Nick was speechless. Phillipe turned slowly, silently taking in the staggering sight. Then, abruptly, he began issuing orders, and his team quickly began planting explosives around the eggs.

"We do not have enough dynamite," Jean-Claude reported a few minutes later.

Nick was about halfway up the destroyed bleachers, studying a group of eggs. Wading through heaps of fish, Phillipe hurried to the young scientist.

Several yards away, Animal and Audrey reached the arena. Climbing through the hole in the floor, their hands raw from gripping the cable, they came out behind a pile of the enormous reptilian eggs. Before Audrey had even gotten to her feet, Animal raised the videocam to his shoulder and began filming.

"What are all these?" Audrey wondered, glancing around, shocked. "Eggs," she whispered a second later. "There are so many of them."

Phillipe hadn't noticed the intruders. Neither had any of his men, who were busy planting the last of the dynamite. "Nick, we have a problem," he said, climbing the broken bleachers.

Nick's ear was pressed against the shell of an egg.

There was a loud splintering noise.

And then the egg began to crack. A jagged break split its shell.

Nick and Phillipe jumped back, startled. The huge egg rattled as the embryo inside it awakened.

More eggs began to crack. The two men turned and saw shells breaking all around them.

Below them, on the floor of the arena, work halted.

Jean-Claude scrambled to his feet. Pierre set down his bag of explosives. Jean-Luc's hand reached for his gun. One by one, the assault team backed slowly away from the cracking eggs.

Hidden in the forest of tall eggs, Audrey backed away, too.

Only Animal waded forward. Camera on his shoulder, he moved closer, videotaping the hatching eggs.

Suddenly the egg behind Nick and Phillipe exploded. They whirled, stunned, as a terrible small version of the enraged lizard burst from its shell. The small yet powerful creature let out a chilling wail.

A few feet away, another egg burst. Another spinetingling cry announced the birth of a terrifying new beast. "The babies," Jean-Claude shouted. "They are alive!"

The unearthly shrieks and sounds of shells breaking suddenly seemed to come from every corner of the arena. For the moment, the scaly, wet creatures busied themselves gobbling up the dead fish laying all around them.

"I think we should leave now," Phillipe said softly, backing carefully down the bleacher steps.

"Good idea," Nick agreed.

They moved as silently as possible between the rattling eggs and splattering shells, toward the exit. Phillipe took out his radio. "Everyone, outside! Now!" he commanded.

Jean-Claude and Jean-Luc glanced at one another. Pierre ran to warn another team of men who were still laying down explosives.

One of the newly hatched creatures watched him. Then it

let a half-eaten fish fall to the floor and started after the young Frenchman.

"Animal," Audrey hissed. "Let's get out of here!"

"One more second," Animal insisted, continuing to shoot a cracking egg. "This is fantastic."

Behind Audrey, a Baby Godzilla, fish hanging from its jaw, began to move toward them.

"Don't you think we have enough?" Audrey urged.

Animal glanced at her and saw the small, alert creature approaching. "Yes. Definitely," he said, watching the beast. "Definitely enough."

Audrey turned to see what Animal was staring at. Her eyes widened. She backed up, bumping into Animal. Another creature suddenly appeared on the other side of them.

"Just be calm," Animal whispered. "Don't startle them." He led her backwards, toward the large hallway at the end of the floor. It was the players' entrance, the tunnel through which the sports teams entered the arena.

Somewhere inside it there were dressing rooms and, Animal hoped, an exit to the street. If the giant lizard hadn't demolished that section of the arena . . .

Eggs were cracking all around them. The two babies had finished their fish and begun to sniff the air. Audrey tiptoed backwards.

An egg splintered next to her. A scaly arm broke out of the shell, grabbing at her leg. Claws pinched her ankle. She screamed.

Animal began battering the powerful arm with his flashlight. Frantically, Audrey kicked free of the creature. They both took off running.

"Lock the doors shut!" Phillipe called into the radio. "We

107

must keep them contained inside." Behind him, Nick whipped off his belt and wrapped it around the door handles, clamping them closed.

At the opposite end of the enormous arena, Jean-Claude and Jean-Luc separated their paths, each of them moving quickly but cautiously toward a different exit door. Others were doing the same. All around them, the newborns were feasting on fish.

An egg cracked as Pierre and two of the men he had alerted, Alain and Vincent, hurried past it.

Screeching with hunger, the creature that popped out of the egg sniffed the air. Its head whirled toward the men. "Oh, no," Alain whispered. "He smells us."

"He wants fish," Pierre assured him.

"Yes," Vincent said in a panic, "and that is what we smell like!"

It was true, Pierre realized as the baby began to run at them. The trio raced for the exit along the wet, littered floor. Godzilla's children were everywhere now, springing up the bleacher aisles, and fighting over mounds of fish.

Vincent slipped and called out to Alain. Alain turned back to help him up. Before he reached his fallen teammate, one of the beasts pounced onto his back, piercing his skin with razor-sharp claws.

Vincent scrambled to his feet, gripping a piece of lead pipe he'd grabbed from the floor. Pierre tore a leg mount off one of the broken seats. Together, they beat the screeching beast off Alain's back, then half-carried, half-dragged the wounded man to the exit. They slammed the door shut behind them, bolting it with the piece of pipe.

Audrey and Animal had reached the team entrance. They

raced through it to the street exit. Audrey tugged at the doors. They were locked.

A piercing cry echoed through the concrete passageway. Audrey spun around. Three of the creatures were at the very end of the tunnel, blocking their return to the arena. And Animal was shouldering his videocam again, preparing to film them!

She looked around frantically. There was a locker room halfway down the tunnel. She grabbed Animal's arm and dragged him toward it. Miraculously, it was open. As the wailing beasts rushed at them, Audrey and Animal ducked inside, slammed the door, and locked it.

They barely had time for a sigh of relief when the door was battered by a series of jolting thuds. The newborn beasts were trying to get in. "Great," Audrey said, leaning against a table and trying to catch her breath. "Now what do we do?"

"There's got to be another way out of here," Animal said frantically.

The door was jarred again. One of its hinges began to come loose. Audrey threw back her head and closed her eyes. A second later, her eyes shot open. She was staring at a ceiling vent.

"Come on," she ordered Animal, who was piling benches against the door. "Help me move this table." She climbed up and yanked out the grate covering the air vent. "Think we can fit up in there?" she asked.

"Only one way to find out," Animal said, rushing over to help her climb into the vent.

In one of the hallways circling the arena, Nick and Phillipe raced from door to door, doing their best to lock the raging creatures inside. In the corridors above and below them, teams of Phillipe's men were doing the same. Several of them had had encounters with the babies. Not all of the men had survived.

Alain was one of the lucky ones. He was still in pain from the clawing he'd received. His own blood mingled with the fish blood, scales, and entrails soaking through his uniform. Still, once the shock had passed, he'd been able to keep up with Pierre and Vincent as they circled the lower level of the arena, locking doors.

The auditorium was filled with hatched beasts devouring and fighting over the remaining fish, and looking around uneasily for more to eat. One of the scaly creatures reared its ropy neck and stared at Nick and Phillipe. Its nostrils opened, taking in their scent.

Suddenly the baby sped up the aisle toward them.

Phillipe slammed the door. Nick smashed the glass cover of a nearby fire hose and wrapped it around the door handles. A moment later, a loud thud sounded as the hungry beast began to throw itself against the locked door.

Phillipe tossed his cellular phone to Nick. "Contact the military. Get them to send a bomber to blow up this building before these things escape," he hollered, racing to secure the next exit.

"How do I do that?" Nick called.

"Dial 555-7600. Tell them it's a Code Dragonfly. That should get you through."

"Amazing," Nick muttered, staring after him.

"What are you waiting for?" Phillipe shouted.

Nick dialed. "All circuits are busy right now," an automated voice informed him. "Please hang up and try again."

He did. He dialed the number four more times and

then tried 911 and then dialed Operator. All of the lines were busy.

"I can't get through." Nick chased after Phillipe. The banging on the doors was increasing. Soon one of them would give.

Jean-Claude arrived with half a dozen others. Their uniforms were soaked and bloody. "We've secured the doors on the upper levels," he announced.

"Where are my other men?" Phillipe asked.

Jean-Claude looked away. "They didn't make it," he said.

Phillipe nodded. "Nick, my men and I will hold them here. You will have to go and get help."

Nick nodded in agreement and took off down the stairs. Behind him, Phillipe's team snapped together their automatic rifles, preparing for the fight.

On the main floor of the auditorium, Jean-Luc and two others circled the hallway, heading for their posts. "Get the other exits. I'll guard these two doors," the tall, thin Frenchman ordered.

As his men disappeared around the bend, Jean-Luc rushed over to double-check the locked doors. He stopped dead in his tracks as he noticed that one of them was broken. Wide open, it hung crookedly from a single hinge.

The secret agent turned slowly to look down the hall. As he did, a half-dozen screeching beasts appeared. Before he could react, they pounced. Jean-Luc fired his automatic, but he was overrun in a flash.

"Jean-Luc! What's happened?" Jean-Claude called. He was at his post, one landing above. "Jean-Luc?" Suddenly the door behind Jean-Claude collapsed. A wave of ravenous creatures flooded out into the corridor, stampeding him.

The doors were not holding. The hallways were filling with the frantic beasts. Nick was at street level, racing toward the exit, when a nearby door burst open and a herd of them thundered toward him.

He skidded around a corner and saw the elevator straight ahead. There was no choice, nowhere to run. Slamming the elevator call button, he yelled, "Come on, come on!"

The babies sniffed the air and moved toward him from both sides. "This is so not good," Nick muttered, pumping the button.

Just then the elevator doors opened. Nick leaped inside and frantically pushed the "Close Door" button. The elevator's response was painfully slow. "These things never work!" he hollered over the screeching cries of the hungry babies.

One of the creatures leaped forward as the doors finally began to shut. A beaded head, its yellow eyes glaring, its iron jaw wide and howling, got stuck in the closing doors.

Panicked, Nick kicked it. The beast fell back. The doors shut. Nick pressed a button and the car began to rise to the next floor.

The doors opened. Standing directly in front of the elevator, a dozen creatures milled about. They turned at the scent. "Oops, wrong floor," Nick muttered, slamming the button again.

The doors closed in time and the elevator lifted. At the next stop, Nick waited, his hands knotted into fists, his legs prepared to spring and kick.

Phillipe was standing guard. At the sound of the elevator stopping, he swerved his gun around ready to shoot.

"Hey, it's me!" Nick shouted as the doors opened. Pulling the cell phone from his pocket, he dialed again, trying to get through to the command center. The number was still busy.

"They're loose," he told Phillipe, "They're all over the place. I can't get out of the building."

Suddenly there was a fierce rattling overhead. He looked up. Phillipe raised his automatic. "They're in the vents," Nick shouted, panicked.

Just then the grate in the ceiling collapsed. A video camera crashed to the floor. Animal and Audrey tumbled out. In a flash, Phillipe had his weapon trained on their heads. "Who are you?" he demanded.

"It's okay," Nick said. "I know her."

12

An angry mob swarmed behind the roadblock at the Brooklyn Bridge. Television cameras scanned the crowd. Reporters stuck microphones into irate faces. It was the same at the Lincoln and Holland tunnels. Their cars packed with belongings, people were demanding to be let back into Manhattan.

"Godzilla's dead," a man called out.

"It said on the radio they torpedoed him," a furious woman shouted, "so why can't we go home?"

"Why can't we go home?" Suddenly Charles Caiman's face filled the screen. "That's what millions of New Yorkers are asking now that word has leaked out of the death of Godzilla, the beast that stalked New York."

"Godzilla?" Watching Caiman's broadcast on one of the six television screens in the command center, Elsie Chapman shook her head, annoyed. "Who is that yutz?"

"He's with WIDF," Mendel Craven started to answer, but at that moment the mayor of New York slammed down the phone and shoved him out of the way, trying to get to Colonel Hicks.

"Do you have any idea what's going on out there?" the mayor ranted. "The phones are ringing off the hook with people screaming to get back into the city."

Hicks was at the map table, surrounded by smiling generals and admirals. "We're sending divers into the river now to retrieve the body," he replied. The top brass were in a good mood, taking turns congratulating themselves. Only Hicks seemed uncertain of the victory.

"That thing's dead," the mayor pressed. "What are we waiting for?"

Hicks didn't know himself. He wished Tatopoulos hadn't pulled that dumb stunt. He needed Nick's input now. Elsie rushed over. "Colonel, we've got to begin the search for the nest," she reminded him.

"You know that hasn't been approved," Hicks said softly.

"What if Nick is right and we blow this thing?" she insisted.

"There is no nest!" It was the mayor. "Come on, come on!" he barked, his fleshy face turning red. "Open Manhattan, Hicks. It's over."

The fierce newborns were clawing at the bolted doors. Phillipe's eyes shifted briefly toward the noise. Then, facing Animal again, he lowered his gun. "You are a television reporter?" he asked.

"No way," Animal replied. "I'm a cameraman."

"I see." Phillipe pointed his gun at the fallen video camera and fired, ripping the camera apart.

"Hey!" Animal yelled.

"No pictures," Phillipe said.

"What are you doing here?" Nick asked Audrey.

"I thought you said there'd only be a dozen eggs," she said irritably.

"I was wrong," he confessed.

Fierce thudding rattled one of the doors Phillipe had been guarding. They all jumped at the sound. The uproar grew more urgent.

"Do you have a radio, a walkie-talkie?" Phillipe asked, spinning toward the clamor with his weapon aimed at the door. "Anything we can use to contact the outside?"

The locked metal door shuddered. They started backing away from it, moving deeper into the corridor.

"What about the phones?" Audrey asked.

"The circuits are overloaded," Nick explained.

"I know how you can get a message out of here," she said after a moment.

The door burst open. A herd of babies stampeded into the hallway. "This way," Audrey hollered. She took off running. Phillipe and Nick followed. Animal hung back. He darted over to the destroyed videocam and pulled out the tape. Seconds before the screeching creatures trampled the ruined camera, he sprinted after the others.

Bolting door after door behind them, the men trailed Audrey through narrow corridors and up damaged stairways, past the luxury boxes overlooking the auditorium, to a booth filled with broadcasting equipment.

"How'd you know about this?" Nick asked as they locked themselves inside the control room. Its huge window offered a frightening view of the horrors below, the trashed arena filled with frenzied creatures frantically searching for food.

"Our network covers the Ranger games," Audrey reported, sitting down behind a huge console. "We've got a direct feed into our computer system."

"Which means we can contact your station, but they won't

be able to get through to the military any more than I did," Nick reasoned as Phillipe and Animal shoved equipment against the door, securing it.

"When you worked with the military," Animal said to Nick, "they monitored news broadcasts, didn't they?" Nick nodded. "Okay, then." Animal threw his coat to the floor and started checking out the TV cameras in the booth. "We'll go live! We'll broadcast from here and pray that your pals at command central are watching."

The WIDF news truck was parked in the shadow of the Brooklyn Bridge. Inside the van, at the editing console, Ed Mullins was watching Caiman's live broadcast on a small monitor.

"Yes, the threat is over, but the pain continues," the newsman was saying when the computer in the editing bay started beeping.

Ed slid his chair over to it and glanced at the monitor. NEW MAIL: URGENT! it read. He double-clicked and a letter popped up instructing him to turn on the feed from Madison Square Garden. "There's no Ranger game tonight," he muttered, switching on a blank TV screen.

And there was Audrey Timmonds! She was pacing in front of a camera, looking like death on toast. "If you're seeing this, Ed, please put us on live," she was saying.

No way, Ed thought.

"This is urgent," Audrey raved. "I know it sounds crazy, Ed, but you have to do it. Please, trust me —"

There was a lot of weird noise behind her.

Then someone in the background said, "He's not going to do it."

The voice Ed heard was Nick's. He and Phillipe were watching a small TV that showed Charles Caiman still broadcasting from the bridge.

"Oh, yes, he will," Animal promised. He swung his camera off Audrey and pointed it out the control booth window at the rioting beasts below.

In the news truck, Ed's eyes nearly popped out of his head.

"Ed, you see that?" Audrey was saying. "They'll be all over the city if we don't stop them."

The stunned editor rushed over to his console and went to work.

The mood in the command tent was festive. The generals were preparing to leave. Hicks hadn't promised anything, but the mayor was sure the stubborn colonel had gotten his message, loud and clear.

Sergeant O'Neal and some of his men were watching the news. They cheered as Charles Caiman announced, "Fears have been allayed thanks to the dedicated work of our boys in uniform."

Mendel was watching the broadcast, too. He wished he believed there was something to cheer about. Suddenly the smug newsman's image was replaced. "Are we on?" a young woman was asking. "Are we live?"

Plaster dust matted the girl's hair and freckled her distraught face. Her clothes were in tatters. She cleared her throat, and said, "I'm Audrey Timmonds of WIDF-TV. We're live from inside Madison Square Garden, where Dr. Niko Tatopoulos has discovered the beast's lair. Doctor, tell us what is happening here."

"*Shhhh*. Hold it," O'Neal quieted his men.

Elsie turned from her charts to the TV monitors again.

Suddenly Nick appeared on the screen, looking even more

119

disheveled than the girl who'd introduced him. "We've discovered over two hundred eggs, which began hatching only moments ago," he said.

There were sounds behind him, thumping, screeching noises.

Listening to them gave O'Neal goose bumps. He moved forward in his seat, straining to hear more clearly.

Mendel leaped up and hurried across the room to Hicks. "You'd better see this," he said.

The colonel crossed to the bank of television screens. "If the military is listening, they must immediately destroy this building before they escape," he heard Nick say.

Then someone in the broadcast booth screamed, "Oh, no, they're coming!" It was the reporter, O'Neal thought. Abruptly, the camera swerved. Through the side window of the broadcast booth they saw dozens of crazed, yowling replicas of the great beast they had torpedoed.

"If those creatures escape and multiply," Nick was warning, "in a very short time a new species will emerge. One that could replace us as the dominant species of this planet."

Colonel Hicks raced to the phone. "Code Dragonfly," he shouted.

O'Neal scrambled to his feet. His men followed. The mayor rushed over to Hicks. "Isn't that the wacko you fired?" he demanded, pointing at the TV screen. "Are you going to believe him?"

"That's correct," Hicks was saying into the phone, "I want you to blow up Madison Square Garden. No, I'm not crazy!" He pushed past the mayor and rushed back to the TV monitors. "What's happening now?" he asked Elsie. "Where's Nick?"

Her eyes were wide with fear, and quickly filling with tears. "Getting out of there fast, I hope," she said.

Hicks looked at the screen. The camera was focused on one of the Garden's luxury booths. It was filled with screeching, scrambling little monsters clawing over one another in their rage to get to the broadcast booth. Standing with her back to that terrifying scene, the brave young announcer was urging them to bomb the building.

Phillipe had stayed in the background, out of camera range. Now that Animal's lens was focused on the attacking mutants, he leaped into action.

Grabbing a large spool of coaxial cable from a corner of the booth, the secret agent began tying it around a support beam. Nick ran to his aid.

"Regardless of what happens to us," Audrey was saying, "the important thing is that this place is destroyed before they can escape out into the city. Hopefully we can contain the spread of these creatures here." She glanced over her shoulder at the warring predators, and tried to stop trembling. "Reporting live from Madison Square Garden," she said quickly, "this is Audrey Timmonds, WIDF."

Animal lowered the camera. Everyone in the booth was silent.

Suddenly the computer began beeping. Animal lunged at it and read the incoming note. "The good news is they got the message," he told them. "The bad news is we've got five and a half minutes to get out of the building."

The room rocked as babies began crashing against the blocked door.

Phillipe tugged at the fastened cable, then jumped to his

feet. "Okay, the party is over," he announced. "It is time to leave." With that, he sprayed bullets into the front window, shattering it. Glass rained down below. Phillipe tossed the spool of cable out the broken window. "Anyone care to join me?" he asked.

Animal ripped one of the video cameras from its stand. Hoisting it to his shoulder, he joined Phillipe. The grizzled agent slid down the cable, then covered Animal as he shinnied down from the broadcast booth.

Audrey and Nick stared nervously at the long drop. The door behind them was beginning to give way. Suddenly Audrey leaned over and kissed Nick. "In case I can't later," she explained. Grasping the cable, she jumped out and rappelled downward.

Stunned by the unexpected kiss, Nick watched her. The sound of the door splintering brought him back to his senses. As the bellowing babies flooded into the room, Nick jumped.

With Phillipe in the lead, firing at everything that moved, they raced into the main lobby.

At the top of the busted escalator, they froze. Below them, a herd of babies were tearing apart a concession stand, fighting over stale popcorn and candy bars.

One by one the raging beasts stopped, began to sniff the air, and slowly looked up.

"How much time do we have?" Audrey whispered.

Nick checked his watch. "Sixty seconds."

Three large chandeliers hung in a direct line between them and the front door. Phillipe fired a short burst at the first, slicing the cable that supported it.

The fixture dropped, shattering at the bottom of the escalator. Startled, the creatures staring up at them scattered.

"So, let's go." Phillipe led the dash down the broken escalator. Midway down, he shot the next chandelier. It crashed, too, clearing a path to the exit.

They were a few feet from the doors when the scattered babies began charging again.

Nick grabbed a candy machine and threw it back at the oncoming creatures. The glass globe shattered. Thousands of gum balls rolled across the floor.

The shrieks and bellows became deafening as one after another the enraged beasts slid, stumbled, and fell over the gum balls.

The sound of jet fighters filled the air above the Garden. The last chandelier quivered and clattered. Phillipe shot it down. "Go, go, go!" the French agent urged as they dashed past him, out into the night.

Audrey and Nick raced away from the doomed building. Animal waited for Phillipe. With a final burst of gunfire, the Frenchman backed out. Animal pulled the doors shut behind him as the babies charged again. Phillipe slid his rifle barrel between the handles as a temporary lock. Then he pulled Animal away and they ran.

The street rattled in the wake of the bombers. Shrieking missiles rained down. An enormous explosion erupted, engulfing the entire arena in a mountain of flame.

The force of the impact threw the runners forward, toppling them to the ground. Phillipe skidded across the concrete, face-first. Animal tumbled after him. As the building crumbled, flames crackling, they could hear the screams of the thrashing beasts.

Moments later, there was only silence.

13

Nick sat up slowly and turned to Audrey. "Are you okay?" he asked, touching her cheek gently.

She was shaking. She nodded and laughed. "Somehow I never thought your life was this exciting."

"You'd be surprised," he said, grinning.

Phillipe's cheek was bleeding. Animal examined the cut on the agent's bearded face. "You all right, man?"

"I could use a coffee," Phillipe joked.

As Animal helped him up, the street suddenly began to vibrate. The few bits of glass still trapped in window panes clattered fiercely.

A rumbling sounded underground.

It was followed by a ghastly wail, an ear-shattering shriek of rage.

Violently bursting up through the remains of Madison Square Garden, through the ashes and smoking timber, the mammoth beast appeared.

"Godzilla!" Animal whispered.

Bleeding from his wounds, the mutant lizard leaned down and nuzzled the burnt-out remains of his nest.

Audrey felt her heart lurch. It was fear, of course. And something else. There was an awful expression on the monster's face as he searched for his young. It was a look, Audrey thought, of terrible pain.

That pain turned quickly to burning rage. The huge head swung downward, staring directly and accusingly at them.

"He looks angry," Nick whispered.

"So what do we do?" Animal asked.

"Run," Phillipe advised.

And they did, darting down an alleyway just as the furious beast pounced.

Without hesitating, the towering creature bulldozed into the narrow alley, ripping the buildings apart as he plowed forward.

Glancing over her shoulder, Audrey stumbled. Nick rushed back to help her up. Bricks flew and debris showered down on them as they raced to join Phillipe and Animal, who had made it through.

Dashing out of the alley, Phillipe sprinted over to a parked yellow cab. In one move, he drew a screwdriver out of his belt, popped the ignition device off the steering column, and hotwired the car. It took less than fifteen seconds.

"Man, you're good," Animal said, holding the door open as Nick and Audrey piled in. As soon as the engine turned over, with Animal barely inside, Phillipe hit the gas and took off.

The immense beast burst from the alleyway into their path. There was no time to turn. The cab hit one of Godzilla's huge toenails like a ramp and went airborne. It landed hard, skidding around the corner.

The enraged monster was right behind it. His huge frothing jaws snapped at the cab, but Phillipe gunned the motor, swerving just out of danger.

As the taxi lurched through the ruined streets, Animal filmed out the back window. "Better step on it, Frenchie!" he warned as the creature closed the gap between them.

With incredible skill and more than a little luck, Phillipe zigzagged through the city streets.

Twice more the jagged teeth snapped at the taxi, coming so close that the car windows fogged. Windshield wipers flapping, the taxi careened through an intersection.

"Look out!" Audrey hollered.

There was a wild screeching of brakes behind them.

Led by Sergeant O'Neal, a military convoy was racing for Madison Square Garden. Flying into the intersection, the sergeant slammed on his brakes to avoid plowing into the passing cab. The armored vehicles behind him rammed into one another.

"What was that?" O'Neal blurted, staring after the out-of-control cab.

The street beneath the stalled convoy shook. O'Neal looked up.

"Godzilla!" one of his men yelled.

A giant foot smashed down on the hood of one of the trucks. The soldiers dived for safety as the beast passed, racing after the cab.

O'Neal grabbed the radio off his belt. "Command, Command, find Colonel Hicks," he called. "Godzilla is back!"

Nick looked back at the soldiers.

"That was O'Neal," he said. "Turn around."

"Are you crazy?" Phillipe hollered.

Nick reached over and ripped the cab's license off the dashboard. "Do it!" he ordered.

Phillipe swerved the cab around. The beast was running

toward them at full speed. The taxi roared through its massive legs.

O'Neal had reached Hicks. The colonel was radioing his F-18 bombers, ordering them back into action. Recovering from the crash, O'Neal's men were trying to repair their trucks when the taxi returned. It was heading straight for them again. And the beast was behind it.

The soldiers dived back into their vehicles.

Leaning out of the speeding cab, Nick tossed out the taxi license.

O'Neal scrambled to pick it up. CAB #MN44, it read. "Excellent," the sergeant muttered appreciatively. "Very slick."

Minutes later, he led his convoy into a deserted taxi garage. Breaking into the dispatch room, he searched frantically through books and paperwork.

"What are we looking for, sir?" one of his soldiers asked.

"They always keep a record of each cab's radio frequency," O'Neal said, flipping through the notebook. "Got it!" He slapped the right page.

Across town, with the beast snapping at its rear bumper, the cab veered wildly onto Park Avenue.

There was a construction blockade in front of the express tunnel, an underground road that ran for six blocks beneath the usually busy avenue. "In there!" Nick shouted.

The taxi burst through the blockade and dove into the tunnel. A second later, the giant reptile jammed its head into the underground passage.

"Go!" Nick yelled, staring out the back window. "Gun it."

Suddenly Phillipe slammed on the brakes. Their path was blocked by heavy construction machinery.

They were trapped inside.

"Okay, smart guy," Animal said, "what do we do now?"

"Turn out the lights," Nick ordered.

Phillipe did. They were plunged into total darkness.

"Nick, you there? Hello, come in, Worm Man." The cab's radio crackled to life.

"O'Neal!" Nick grabbed the radio.

"Nice trick. Where are you?" the sergeant asked.

"You've got to help us. We're in . . ."

"Park Avenue midtown tunnel," Audrey told him as the creature began burrowing toward them.

"He's got us trapped in here," Nick said.

"Nick, listen," O'Neal instructed. "Hicks has called in the air strike. But you guys have to lure Godzilla out into the open so we can get a clear shot at him."

Animal gave a sarcastic laugh. "Right," he said. "Want us to wash him up, too?"

"Where's the nearest suspension bridge?" Nick asked suddenly.

"Brooklyn," Audrey said.

"Let's go!" Nick was excited.

"And how would you suggest we do that?" Phillipe gestured to the ferocious head blocking the exit, the claws scrabbling toward them.

"Has this thing got high beams?" Nick asked.

Phillipe understood. He made a quick U-turn and gunned the car. It peeled out, heading directly at the beast. Moments before collision, Phillipe hit the bright lights. Nick slammed his hand down on the horn.

Startled, the huge beast jerked back, splitting the upper section of the tunnel. With asphalt and beams falling, the cab zoomed out. "Downtown!" Audrey hollered. "Take the Drive."

"Nah," Animal objected. "It's always jammed. Take Second Avenue."

"Earth to Animal," Audrey grumbled. "It's not exactly rush hour, is it?" She indicated the torn and empty streets.

Phillipe headed the taxi downtown, barreling through side streets, alleyways, underground garages, any place small and narrow enough to slow the mammoth monster.

"There!" Audrey shouted. The bridge was in sight. The cab sped up the on-ramp.

"I think we lost him," Animal said, looking out from behind his camera. "I don't see him anymore."

"Really?" Nick turned to look out the back window.

With an explosive blast, the on-ramp ripped open. The beast reared up through the concrete only yards ahead of the cab.

Phillipe hit the brakes, but the slippery road sent the taxi spinning into a wild skid. It stopped just under a big highway sign.

Jaws wide, the roaring creature thrust forward to bite down on the cab.

The large steel sign above the car slammed into the roof of his mouth, preventing him from biting down.

The sign supports began to bend under the stress of those powerful jaws. An electric cable came loose and dangled dangerously close to the cab.

"Gun it! Get us out of here!" Audrey shouted as everyone inside ducked.

"I'm trying!" Phillipe assured her as the cab's wheels spun in vain against the gigantic tongue pushing against it.

Like a dog with a bone, the frustrated beast shook his head, determined to tear loose the sign supports and snap his iron jaws shut.

The electric cable swung wildly, sparks shooting from its exposed wires.

Suddenly Nick ripped off his jacket, wrapped it around his hand, and opened the cab door. Grabbing the cable with his wrapped hand, he jammed it down into Godzilla's tongue. There was an explosive burst of fire. Sparks crackled.

Nick fell back inside, slamming the door shut.

Shocked, the beast's mouth flew open. He pulled back his tongue. And the taxi's spinning wheels hit the road.

Landing hard on the pavement, the cab peeled out, burning rubber as it zoomed onto the bridge.

The creature quickly recovered and stepped onto the bridge. The roadway bounced fiercely. The cab went airborne, then bottomed out as it returned to the heaving asphalt beneath it.

Phillipe slowed and swerved, then revved up again. It was like driving through an earthquake.

On either side of them, the great suspension cables that held the bridge stretched and contracted like rubber bands. The huge steel towers they threaded through swayed treacherously. As the beast crashed through the first set of towers, he got caught in the immense cables.

The more he struggled in the big wires, swatting frantically at them, the more entangled he became.

"He's stuck," Animal reported, desperately trying to steady his camera.

Above the bridge, the air was suddenly filled with swooping F-18 fighter jets.

Phillipe floored the gas pedal. The cab soared through the second set of towering girders. They were almost across.

The massive creature bellowed in frustration, fighting to free himself. The cables whipped against his flesh, lashing his immense body again and again. Like a fly in an enormous web, he was frozen in the tangled suspension wires.

The taxi got to the other side of the bridge and slid to a stop. Nick jumped out and looked back at the creature. Audrey came up beside him. Together they watched the desperate beast's terrible struggle.

A moment later the F-18s fired at the immense trapped reptile. The deadly missiles slammed into his chest, exploding. The huge torso ripped apart. The beast bellowed in pain, but kept trying to tear through the cables to free himself.

Audrey covered her eyes. She was crying. Nick wrapped his arms around her.

Again the bombers fired and the missiles screamed. The massive creature was hit again.

Animal kept filming. In back of him, behind the blockade, the mob that had gathered at the bridge watched in horror.

Mortally wounded, the immense beast reared up, screaming. Audrey, Nick, and Phillipe moved back as he began to fall. Even Animal retreated.

Just as they stepped away, the enormous head came crashing down on top of the cab, crushing it completely. The earth shook. Rocked by the impact, the crowd screamed. And then a stunned silence fell.

The creature's last breath escaped. Defeated and weary, his eyes blinked slowly as his life slipped away.

The shocked mob began to stir. There was a smattering of

nervous applause and then scattered shouts and relieved, ecstatic cheering.

"Victor!" a joyful voice called. Animal set down his camera as Lucy burst from the crowd, dashing to him. He caught her in his arms and spun her around. "Don't you ever sneak out on me again!" she scolded, showering him with kisses.

They were mobbed by reporters. News crews rushed through the barricades, screaming questions, cameras rolling.

"There's Tatopoulos," someone cried. Soon Nick and Audrey were surrounded. "Dr. Tatopoulos, did Godzilla have a nest?" a reporter demanded. "Where did he come from?" another shouted. "Can you tell us what happened back there?"

Nick hardly heard them. He was staring at the sad and lifeless face of the mutant lizard. Even as he tried to comfort Audrey, he felt a strange and deep sadness at the sight of the toppled giant.

"Oh, no," Audrey whispered suddenly, moving out of his arms.

"Out of the way! Out of the way. This is a WIDF exclusive, fellows!" Charles Caiman was pushing his way to the front of the mob.

"Who is that guy?" Nick asked as reporters elbowed past one another, competing for his attention.

"He's the one who stole my story — and your tape," Audrey said unhappily.

The questions were coming fast and furiously. "Were you the first to see Godzilla? Where did he come from? Are there more of them? How did you track him down?"

"Sorry, guys." Nick grinned suddenly. "I've promised my story as an exclusive to another reporter."

Caiman sprung from the crowd and ran to Audrey. "We did

it!" he announced. "We've got the exclusive! Audrey, you're beautiful!"

"*We* did?" she said coldly. "I don't think so."

"Audrey, remember you work for me." Caiman strained to hold onto his smile.

"Not anymore, Chuck. I quit," she said.

"Yesss!" It was Lucy. She was hanging onto Animal's arm and laughing like crazy.

A convoy of trucks came over the bridge. Sergeant O'Neal jumped out of the first one and ran up to shake Nick's hand. They were suddenly raked by a ferocious wind as Colonel Hicks's helicopter swooped low over the bridge. "Good job, Worm Man," the colonel's voice boomed from a loudspeaker overhead.

Nick looked up to see Hicks grinning and signaling him with a congratulatory thumbs-up. In the colonel's helicopter, Mendel and Elsie were also smiling triumphantly.

"Audrey?" Animal was checking the pockets of his coat and jacket. "Audrey, did you take the tape out of the camera?" he called to her.

"Where's Phillipe?" Nick asked suddenly.

They looked around. He was gone, nowhere to be seen.

A phone began to ring. Nick patted his pocket and found Phillipe's cellular phone. He clicked it on. "Hello?"

"It's Phillipe," the familiar voice said. "Tell your friends I will send the tape after I remove a few items from it."

"Is it him?" Audrey mouthed. Nick nodded. "I understand," he told the French agent.

"I just wanted to say *au revoir* and thank you for your help, my friend," Phillipe said.

"Wait," Nick urged. But the line went dead. "*Au revoir*," he murmured to himself.

"Who was that Frenchman, anyway?" Audrey asked as they followed O'Neal to his truck.

Nick looked back at the huge vanquished beast, the deadly monster the nuclear bomb tests had created, the "mistake" Phillipe had been sent to clean up. "Just some insurance guy," he said.

Afterword

Madison Square Garden was a mass of smoking wreckage. Weeks after the bombings, cleanup crews could still feel the heat.

Beneath the arena, Penn Station was also filled with smoldering rubble. Train tunnels had collapsed. Some would be shut for months. Others, lost under tons of collapsed concrete and steel, would never be used again.

In one such tunnel, far underground, protected by packed earth and warmed by sizzling embers, a gigantic egg nestled.

As trains rumbled by on the few cleared tracks, the towering egg rocked slightly.

A crack formed in its shell.

It was a very small crack. It might have been made by the vibrations of the trains, or the jackhammers of the cleanup crews high overhead, or other forces outside the egg. But it might also have come from within, from something inside the shell struggling to break free and live.